The Killer's Collection

By Zachary D Ayers

Copyright © 2023 By Zachary D Ayers

All rights reserved. No part of this publication may be reproduced, distributed, or transmitted in any form or by any means, including photocopying, recording, or other electronic or mechanical methods, without the prior consent of the publisher, except in those cases of brief quotations embedded in critical reviews and certain other noncommercial uses permitted by copyright law.

This is a work of fiction. Any names, characters, and/or places are either the product of the author's imagination or are used fictitiously.

Books By Zachary D Ayers

Collection Of Short Stories

The Killer's Collection

Short Stories

Operation Containment

Feral Woods

Acknowledgements of the people who were involved in the creation of The Killer's Collection:

Author - Zachary D Ayers

Story Covers - Zachary D Ayers, Ryan McClusky, and Zoe Thompson

Book Cover - Zachary D Ayers, Ryan McClusky

Proofreader - K Downey

Contents

The Clown's Deception............................7

My Whispering Addiction..........................38

An Abominable Christmas..........................53

My Dangerous Admirer.............................70

The Shadow Man...................................89

Flickering Lamp Post.............................107

The Family Tradition.............................122

ZaKiki Island....................................127

Psych Ward.......................................159

Stay out of the Attic............................198

Prisoner...212

Thee Embedded....................................229

Locked Away......................................246

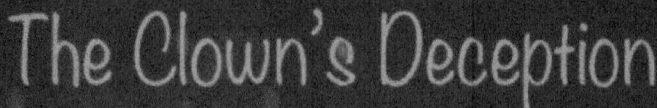

The Clown's Deception
Story Summary

It all started when the Harlem County Fair was shut down back in the 1980's after a ride malfunctioned, resulting in the deaths of 12 people. Forty years later, the theme park was reopened under new management in an attempt to bring the Harlem County fair back to what it once was, the scariest fair in all of New York. The new owner hired dozens of employees, but only one stood out from the rest, Perry the Clown. Perry was just what the fair needed. He was one ugly, overweight man who really appeared to fit the role of a creepy clown; however, it wasn't until management hired an 18-year-old boy named Scott, who had a phobia of clowns, that it was discovered that Perry was more than just a clown.

A New Beginning

Chuck -

I've lived in Harlem all my life, and I've been obsessed with carnivals ever since I was a boy. My favorite fair to go to was the Harlem County Fair. It was the scariest carnival in all of New York. Unfortunately, they closed down when I was just 15 years old. I was so enraged when the fair closed down that I vowed that when I was older, I would attempt to purchase and reopen it. So that's exactly what I did.

I became a successful business man and pulled in enough money to buy the land that the abandoned park sat on. The land wasn't the expensive part, it was getting new and safer rides, and the attraction itself, to lure people to visit and spend their money. I was devoted to ensuring that the fair would become the scariest one in the United States; however, to accomplish that, I would need employees, makeup artists, and regular carnies.

Once the news broke that the Harlem Fair was purchased and reopening, applications started overwhelming my email. It was great so many people were applying, but most were just amateurs. I did end up hiring 30 carnies and 10 staff members, but only four scarers. It was a good first month of recruitment, but just as I thought I was never going to find any more scarers, I received a text message from an unknown number, who introduced himself as Perry.

Perry claimed he was interested in becoming the fair's clown. I wasn't quite sure how to respond, but I sure wasn't going to let the possibility of hiring another scarer fly over my head. So I replied, "Nice to hear from you, Perry. If you're really interested, meet me at the ticket booth at the front of the carnival at midnight". Perry never responded to that text, but I still decided to wait for him. I was hopeful that he would still show up. I sat inside the ticket booth and waited until 11:45 PM.

Scott -

I was entering my senior year at Red Rock High School, and I still didn't have a car. My parents sure weren't going to just buy me one, so that meant I needed a job, and one that paid well. I looked on the help wanted board outside the gymnasium doors, but nothing seemed interesting, and if it was, it paid horribly. It was hopeless. I feared I would never find a job. The bell rang, and I heard the footsteps of students rushing to lunch, but I was too focused on this board to care about eating.

Of course, while I was minding my own business, someone bumped into me, knocking me flat on my ass. I looked up and saw the kid's face. He looked very intimidating, he was tall, muscular, and had long, dirty blonde hair. To my surprise, he apologized and helped me up off the floor. He introduced himself as Bill and claimed that he was new to the area. Bill smiled and then asked if I would join him for lunch. I hesitated, but he offered to pay for it to show he was genuinely sorry for knocking me over. I decided I wasn't going to turn down a free lunch, plus I had no friends, so I said, "Yeah, sure. I'm down."

Bill shouted, "Aye, let's go," and lifted his fist.

I flinched. Bill looked confused and asked, "Oh you guys don't fist bump around here?"

Once I heard Bill say that, I felt like a loser. I decided to break the silence and change the subject.

"Where are we going for lunch?" I asked.

Bill looked at me and said, "You choose, man. I'm new here, remember?"

Somehow that just made me feel even more pathetic. I mentioned a sub place down the street, and I made sure to inform him that I didn't drive yet.

Bill said, "No worries, man. I'll drive."

We walked through the halls and out into the parking lot. Bill pointed to his car and we climbed inside. I will say it wasn't a piece of junk, nor was it anything special. It was just a normal used car. I told him to just take a right out of the parking lot and that the sub shack was a half mile down the road. Bill said nothing and just continued driving down the road. There was a brief silence as he pulled into the parking lot.

Bill grabbed his keys, locked his car, and headed toward the front doors. As we walked in, he joked, "Ah, I wonder if they're hiring here?" We both laughed and made our way to the front of the line. There was only one person working, and she seemed to hate her life. I didn't get anything absurd or complicated. I just got the classic steak and cheese sub with lettuce and chipotle sauce.

Bill ordered a Buffalo chicken sub, which made my steak sub look unappetizing. I won't lie, Bill ordered my favorite sub, though I decided not to order that one because it was more expensive, and the total already came to $28.56. While Bill paid, I grabbed our drinks. Then I looked around to find a table. I chose one right next to the window and put our stuff there, and while Bill was getting napkins, I strolled over to the bathrooms.

I took a quick leak, washed my hands, and left. While I was walking back towards the table, I saw Bill just completely staring at a TV in the corner of the dining room. I was curious and decided to take a look at what he was watching. Bill appeared to be watching the news.

The headlines were about the Harlem County Fair making its first appearance since it was shut down decades ago. Bill seemed really excited and so did I since the new owner was looking for employees, and the jobs paid anywhere from $12-20 an hour. The ad said if you are interested, shoot Chuck Morris an email, and he'll send you an application. I was stoked. Literally an interesting job that could pay well had basically fallen in my lap. I looked back at Bill. I asked him what he thought; he described it as "radical" and said he planned on applying. So once we finished eating, we searched up Chuck Morris, and we both sent an email for an application. I gestured a high five. Bill got the hint and said, "Gnarly, man!"

Phobia

Scott -

We got up and threw out our trash. On the way towards the car, we saw a really creepy looking man who was enormous and walked really slowly. He had a clown outfit on, torn and dirty, and he held a duffle bag. He must have felt our gaze because he stopped and turned toward us.

As we got into Bill's car, the clown stuck his thumb up. I told Bill we should probably go now, but he insisted we help the guy out. Now would probably be a good time to mention I have had a phobia of clowns ever since I attended my first carnival. They are just so weird and creepy. I started to have flashbacks of the first time I saw a clown, but it quickly faded as I heard Bill say, "Hey, man. Do you need a ride?" The clown just stared at us, then tilted his head and nodded.

Bill told him he could sit in the back. The man was so big he barely fit in the back seat. Once we all were inside, Bill asked, "Where ya headed"? There was a long pause before the man's raspy voice grunted, "the Harlem Fair." That completely ruined my day. Of course the job that I finally wanted would be the same job this freak was applying for. I wasn't surprised that Bill was thrilled, as he said, "No way! Us too, dude!"

I looked in the rearview mirror and watched as he turned his head towards the window. Even though I was petrified, I managed to ask, "So what's your name?" He didn't break his gaze from the window, so I asked again. His head snapped back towards me, and he frowned. He reached in his little old crappy duffle bag, pulled out a card, and handed it to me. I read the card and said, "Oh, your name's Perry? That's cool." Perry just stared at me and chuckled; it sounded horrific, and then, of course, he smiled.

We finally arrived at the Harlem Fair gates. Thankfully, they were still open. Bill and I jumped out of the car and saw a nicely dressed figure sitting in the front of a ticket booth.

We made our way to the man in front of the ticket booth, and he put out his hand, introducing himself as Chuck Morris! I thought to myself there's no way it was actually him. Chuck smiled, and it immediately made my day. We mentioned we were interested in a job. He took a quick look at us and said, "You're hired." We shook hands with him, and

I made sure to thank him. Of course, just as quickly as my day became amazing, it went to hell as Chuck took his attention from us back toward the car. Mr. Morris asked, "Is he with you?" He was talking about the clown. I stuttered, "Ugh, no, not really sir," but that's when Bill opened his big mouth, claiming, "Oh yeah, that's our buddy, Perry." Chuck's eyes widened so that it looked like his pupils were even smiling, and he ran past us to greet Perry.

Mr. Morris told Perry he was late, but he was still glad he made it. I watched as he put out his hand, suggesting a handshake; however, Perry looked at him creepily and just asked if was hired. Chuck, without hesitation, informed him he was, and that he would even get paid top dollar since he already appeared to be the creepiest scarer. In the middle of Chuck's response, Perry turned around and started walking toward the woods. He stopped at the tree line, turned back, and slowly waved as he disappeared into the woods.

In the back of my mind, I was wondering what the fuck just happened. Right before the question left my mouth, Chuck screamed, "Perry, where are you going?" Bill looked confused and asked, "You guys think he lives in the woods?" Chuck glanced at Bill, replying that Perry was obviously just showing off his talent, and he was sure he would return by the weekend when the fair was to be reopened. Mr. Morris asked if we had any talents, and we both

just looked at him funny. We watched as he stroked his beard, until he finally said he had an idea.
He told us he thought we would make a great duo, and we could operate the ferris wheel. Bill asked, "How much are we getting paid?" Mr. Morris thought about it for a second, then asked, "How does $14.50 an hour sound?" We both simultaneously said that would be great! He told us that since we would be operating the rides, we needed to be trained. He then added that training started tomorrow at 3 PM. I assured him that we would be there. Before we left, he mentioned how we would receive our uniforms the day after training ended. Chuck wished us a good day and started heading to a small building, which looked like an office. Bill and I watched until he was completely inside before we made our way to the car.

On the way back, I asked Bill how he wasn't creeped out by Perry. Bill just replied that he never judges a book by its cover. If I'm being honest, I know it had barely been a day, but I had a feeling Bill and I would become good friends. I admired his positive energy. We drove around a bit longer, and then I realized it was dinner time. I decided to ask Bill if he would like to come over to my house for dinner. He said, "For sure man, thanks"! I laughed and said, "No problem, bro." I told him the way to my house, and we got there in only about five minutes.

Bill pulled into my driveway, parked behind my sister's car, and we got out. I grabbed my house key from my pocket and unlocked the front door. As we stepped in, I called out, informing the whole house that a friend of mine was joining us for dinner. I heard laughter in response. It was my sister; she came trampling down the stairs and said "I don't see anyone." Just as she said that, Bill introduced himself. "Hi, I'm Bill. Nice to meet you." My sister froze. I think she was in shock due to the fact I actually made a friend. That's when things got weird; she started flirting with him the rest of the night and wanted to sit across from him at dinner.

While we were sitting at the table, my parents introduced themselves. I didn't want them interrogating him, so I quickly asked them what's for dinner. They said that was a good question; my mother glanced at Bill and asked, "Bill, what would you like?" Bill claimed he would eat anything. It's funny because little did he know that they would take him very seriously. My mom started cooking while my dad began setting the table. Fortunately, my parents ended up making their signature chicken sandwiches, which are to die for! Anyway, Bill made sure to thank everyone, including me, for the dinner.

As he made his way to the door, I caught up with him and asked if he could drive me to work tomorrow. He said, "Yeah, for sure, man" and gave me a fist bump. I watched as he pulled out of the driveway and turned on the road. Once Bill had started driving away, I accused my sister of having a crush on my new friend. She didn't deny it. My parents asked how I had met him, so I told them everything. After I informed them, I felt tired and decided I was going to go to bed. I was so exhausted from the day. I wished everyone goodnight, walked to my room, got into bed, and fell into a deep sleep.

Nightmare

Scott -

It was the first day of training, and Bill was running late to pick me up. I thought it was weird so I gave him a call, but he didn't answer. Okay, now I was really getting concerned. As much as I was worried about Bill, I really needed to get to work. I went back inside and told my sister she needed to drive me. She only agreed because I told her that something wasn't right with Bill, and since she had a crush on him, I used it to my advantage. First we stopped by his house.

Before he left last night, he told me where he lived, so I could estimate his ETA. My sister cruised down the street all the way down to Bill's; however, his car wasn't outside. Now I really started to freak out. I forced myself to believe he had just forgotten to get me, which was unlikely, but it could be a possibility. My sister sped like a mad man; she was going close to 100 mph. We arrived just about 10 minutes late, and when we pulled in, we saw Bill's car. We both let out a sigh of relief, and we got out and sprinted to his car. Once we got a few feet away, my sister screamed and I started to cry. There was a hand and a foot and puddles of blood in the back seats and outside the doors. I noticed that there seemed to be a trail of blood leading to the woods, so we followed it. It wasn't until we were a few hundred feet in that we heard him. The sound was traumatizing; it sounded like bones crunching and snapping. We followed the source of the noise, and when we found it, we screamed! Perry was on top of Bill with a saw cutting off his limbs one by one. Bill tried screaming, causing Perry to rip out his tongue. I watched as my sister collapsed and Perry drew his attention to me. He frowned and bolted at me.

The sound of my alarm awoke me from my deep sleep, and I was drenched in sweat. I looked around and realized it was just a dream. I looked at the clock; it was 8:00 AM, which meant I was going to be late to school. I found my sister sleeping in her room, so I shook her vigorously until she woke up. She smacked me and threatened me to never wake her up that early again. I told her I was going to be late to school, but she didn't give a shit. So, I lied and told her if she would drive me to school, I would give her Bill's number. My sister leapt out of her bed and lunged for her keys, screaming "Let's go!" We rushed down the stairs and out the door.

I hopped in on the passenger's side while my sister slammed on the gas pedal like there was no tomorrow. Somehow we made it on time. I thanked my sister and sprinted to my first class. My first period class was on the third floor on the opposite side of the school, so when I burst into the room, of course, I was drenched in sweat. As soon as I entered, everyone just stared at me. I told the teacher I was sorry and took a seat in the back. I got out my notebook to take notes, and the class resumed. Midway through the class, I had to use the restroom, so I grabbed a pass, then left. Once I made it to the guys' bathroom, I looked in the mirror. I froze because I could barely recognize who was in the mirror. I looked like complete shit. I decided to wash my face with cold water, and when I looked back into the mirror, I looked normal.

I sighed and made my way out the bathroom. Just as I exited the bathroom, I collided with someone who screamed and cussed me out. I looked down and noticed her drink had exploded all over her shirt, but she blamed me. I didn't know what to do, so I just ran. I prayed that I could make it to the next period without getting in trouble. It was now second period, so I had gym with Bill. I was hoping to see him, just to confirm I was only dreaming about his death.

The bell rang while I was still in the hall, so I spirited to the classroom, grabbed my stuff, and dashed to the gym. Once I got there, I noticed everyone was there except for Bill. That's when I completely broke down. I rushed to the locker room and grabbed my shit. Just before leaving the locker room, I noticed a card on the ground I picked up; it was Perry's card! I chucked the thing in the trash and ran out the doors. I didn't know what to do or where to go. I didn't have a car, and Bill was my only friend. I didn't know or care, so I just ran down the grass hill. At the bottom of the hill, something caught my eye. A figure in the woods was Perry! He waved to me and walked back into the woods. The last thing I remember was fainting.

I woke up and looked around. I was still in my bed! Wait, what? I had just had a dream. Did I have two dreams in one? I was scared out of my mind, but I realized either way it was just a dream. I grabbed my phone and saw it was already 3:00 PM! I had slept through school, and I had five missed calls, two from Bill and three from unknown numbers. I decided to look at my messages.

There were a few from Bill asking where I was, if I was okay, and if I still needed a ride to work. There was one other text from an unknown number; it said, "Sweet dreams." I yelled and smashed my phone to the ground. I started thinking that this was some kind of prank, and I got really mad. I had to use my sister's phone to call Bill. When he answered, I immediately started to apologize and told him I overslept. I also asked if he could still take me to work. Bill told me that he was already there, and he didn't want to get into trouble for leaving to get me. I told him to buy me some time while I figured out a ride.

I asked my sister, but she straight up said no, so I went into my basement and got out my old bike. It was a piece of shit, but it still worked. I brought the bike out of the garage and peddled until my legs went numb. Since the fair was kind of near the woods, I decided to ride along dirt roads. Finally, I saw the front gates, and I took a sigh of relief. That lasted momentarily. I was about 50 feet away, and I saw Perry. He was standing still, facing the woods. I didn't want to get any closer to him, but I was already running late, so I parked my bike up front. That's when I noticed Perry was slowly turning his head towards me; he was frowning, but then it slowly turned into a demonic smile. He bolted at me, but he stopped once I caught up with everyone walking into the fairgrounds.

The first thing I did was find Chuck and apologize, but he said no worries since he had only just started to train Bill. He took one long glance at me, and asked, "What's your damage?" "Ugh, what?" I replied, Bill said, "He means what's the matter, bro." I explained that I overslept and had to ride my bike here. Chuck laughed and told me he liked my determination. I didn't know how to respond, so I just said thanks. After what seemed like days of just Morris talking, we finally finished our training and Chuck asked us for our measurements. He disappeared into a small office and returned with two uniforms; he tossed them to us, asking, "What do you guys think?" I won't lie, they were sick. They had the names of the ride operators on them. Then I saw the back. There was a creepy ass clown with the fair's name above it.

When we went back to the ferris wheel, I noticed Bill didn't quite get the hang of the controls, so I told him he could scan the tickets before entering and that I would operate the ride. Bill really liked the idea and gave me what he calls a "bro hug." That's when I saw Chuck leading a small group of workers to start setting up a big tent. Turns out it was Perry's tent; of course his tent was right next to us. I saw Perry lurking behind the crew.

He was just staring at me without expression, nor did he even blink; he just stared. I decided to break my gaze from him and looked at Chuck. Chuck called everyone in and told us we were opening Friday night, so get ready, be prepared, and scare the shit out of people. Everyone started clapping. Meanwhile, Perry started slowly clapping and grinned. What a freak.

before he got to him, he collapsed on the ground. I went over to his side, trying to get a response, but he didn't move. I checked for a pulse, and there wasn't one. I leapt away from him and turned towards Bill; however, instead of seeing Bill, I saw Perry. He had a smile on his face and rushed past me. He turned the man over and slapped him, and when he didn't move, Perry took the ax and ripped it from his hand. Perry heaved it above his head and brought it crashing down on the man's skull, splitting it wide open. He started to mumble, then turned his head towards me, and he smiled while he held up his hand to his face. He put up one finger, telling me to shush. I was frozen in disbelief as I watched Perry drag the body back into his tent. I couldn't believe my eyes. It all seemed so real, but it couldn't have been right?

I turned around to find Bill, who was crunched up in a ball, sobbing. I asked if he was okay, but he didn't answer. I told Bill what I saw, and he stopped crying. He looked up at me, and asked if that man was a worker here. I told him I didn't know, but I did know there was a herd of people of all ages making their way toward us. I patted Bill on the back and helped him up. I told him that he needed to get himself together; he sniffled and took out his ticket scanner.

I watched Bill verify each ticket, and when the wheel was full, he gave me the thumbs up, and I started the ride. After an hour of operating the ferris wheel nonstop, I noticed that people who entered Perry's tent didn't seem to come out. There were crowds of people trying to peek into his tent when the power suddenly went out. The carnival was dark, but only seconds later the power was back. The lights all turned on in flashing colors, and the music boomed. When the power went out, a lot of people screamed, but they stopped when they realized it was all part of the plan. I did notice, however, when the lights started flashing that still, no one was leaving Perry's tent. Suddenly, his tent curtains flew open and he stood still, gesturing for people to enter. I was so focused on his tent that I forgot to start the ride. I turned instantly towards the line, but there wasn't one. Apparently, no one wanted to ride the ferris wheel anymore.

I decided to use our 15 minute break now, so I closed the ride until 10 PM. That's when Bill suggested he wanted to see what was in Perry's tent. He wondered what was so scary, and he asked me to join him, but I told him I had to actually use the bathroom. I said I'd meet him back at the ferris wheel at 10 PM, and we would reopen the ride. That's when Bill suggested we should go and check out Perry's tent to find out what was really happening, but I told Bill we should just stay out of it and mind our own business. I had a very bad feeling about the whole situation, and I was too afraid to find out. Bill sighed, and said "Ok, man."

I stared at Perry's tent, and my imagination consumed me. The thought of entering Perry's tent traumatized me. Suddenly a hand grasped my shoulder, causing me to snap back into reality. It was Bill. He looked at me and asked if I was all right. I cleared my throat and told him I was fine, and that I just had to use the bathroom. Bill nodded, so I started looking for the closest bathroom. Luckily, I found one not so far away. While I was in there, I heard screams, but I figured it was just the people getting chased around or something. I was about to wash my hands when static crackled abruptly from my walkie talkie.

I reached for the receiver and asked if Bill was there or needed anything. I heard nothing, so I turned up the volume and heard the creepy music from Perry's tent followed by a painful moan. I rushed back to the tent, bolting inside, determined to save my friend, but once I entered, there was nothing there but creepy looking objects. I saw a few of what looked like shafts, but they were made of bone with a skull on top. I nearly puked when I heard another deep groan. I swallowed nervously and stealthily made my way to the sound.

I came to a dark red curtain, and from the other side I heard the noises again. It took all my courage to yank the curtain open. What I saw traumatized me. Perry was holding a small little shaft with a dull blade attached to it, and he was strangling what seemed to be a college student. I watched as he started to slash the man's body, leaving marks everywhere. What was even worse was why the man was groaning. I saw that his tongue had been severed! Perry stopped mutilating the man, and turned towards me. He revealed a bloody smile, and I watched as he started stabbing the man over and over, causing blood to splatter everywhere in the tent. I tried to run, but I tripped over something sharp; my ankle stung and began gushing blood. I looked behind me. It was one of our security officer's bodies. I tried to stand, but I couldn't. I watched as Perry rose from his victim and started shuffling towards me.

I screamed, but Perry covered my mouth and began strangling me. My vision started to fade, but suddenly, I heard a voice, "Scott?" It was Bill! I was so excited I opened my mouth to speak, but no words came out. Then I noticed my mouth was bleeding. I reached my hand inside of my mouth, and to my horror, I discovered my tongue had been removed. I started to cry because I couldn't get Bill's attention, but then by some miracle, I heard Bill walk towards me. He was on the other side of the curtain. I was never so happy when I saw his hand start to pull it aside.

Just before he finished opening it, I felt something grab me and drag me away into a darker area of the tent. I knew it had to be Perry. I also knew that this would be my only time to escape, so I kicked off both of my shoes and prayed Bill would notice them. I was too far away for Bill to see me, but I saw him. He called my name and shouted, "Where are you?" Tears began to stream down my face again, but just as I hoped I would survive, I was dragged into another section of the tent. I made the loudest grunt I could manage as Perry dragged me away. Just before I lost sight of Bill, I saw him turn towards me, looking into the darkness. He heard me!

Perry finally released me from his grip, and then immediately he sliced my other ankle, so I couldn't walk. I tried to let out a moan, but it was silent. I watched as Perry grabbed a hammer and walked out of the room. I looked around, and I thought I had already seen the worst of it. Then, I realized I had made a terrible mistake. Surrounding me in all directions were the bodies of carnies and a bunch of people who had just been attending the fair. There were a few more hanging from the ceiling on hooks; some were missing limbs, others missing their faces, and there was one with cuts all over it. I watched what looked like fresh blood dripping down.

Fight or Flight

Scott -

I wasn't even done being terrorized by the sights in the room when I heard a sudden crash. I heard Bill's voice yelling my name. I feared that Perry had lured Bill in here to kill us both, so with my remaining strength, I took a bone from one of the bodies, used it as a walking stick, and suddenly found myself at a door. What kind of insane tent was this? I wondered. I reached for a knob, but there wasn't one, so I started banging on the door. limped to the door, hoping Bill would find me. Bill must have heard me as the door flung open, and since I was leaning on it, I fell flat onto my back. Bill looked petrified and asked "What happened?" I tried to warn him about Perry by pointing behind him, but he told me that we needed to get the hell out of here.

Bill helped me back to my feet, and he braced my arm around his shoulder. As we slowly shuffled towards the exit, Perry pushed Bill, knocking us both to the floor. I hit the ground and heard something snap. Pain shot through my arm, and I realized I had broken my arm. At this point if Bill escaped without me, I wouldn't be mad. I was just a lump on a log. But I rolled on my side and saw Perry on top of Bill. Bill was pretty strong, but Perry's bodyweight overwhelmed him, and he started strangling Bill.

Bill got one clean good punch on Perry, causing him to lose his grip. Bill turned on his stomach and tried to make a run for it, but by the time he got to his feet, Perry jammed a rusty blade in his back and started violently twisting it back and forth. Bill collapsed and blood was gurgling from his mouth. He tried to speak, but then Perry reached in his mouth and ripped his tongue. Perry held Bill's tongue high above his head while Bill squirmed. I watched as Perry let go of the tongue and let it fall into his mouth. I wanted to yell, "You fucking bastard! Leave him alone!" but nothing actually came out. Perry stopped and looked at me; he smirked and continued stabbing Bill to death.

I just wanted to die, but I wouldn't let myself. I had to avenge Bill. I rolled on to my broken arm and grasped a shaft. I used it to help me stand and I hobbled out of the tent. I could hear Perry's footsteps coming after me, but I had already made it out. Once I got out, I was face to face with Chuck. He looked at me, and I could see the fear in his eyes as he put his hand on my shoulder and asked me what happened. I cried because I could not speak; I would never speak again. Chuck asked where Bill was. I turned to point in the tent, and there stood Perry. He was drenched in blood, but his face was different. He had cut off parts of Bill's face and stitched them onto his own. Perry just stared at me. Chuck noticed and started interrogating Perry. Just as he got within a few feet of him, Perry attempted to grab him, but Chuck dodged it. Chuck grabbed a sharp bone from the outside of Perry's tent and drove it into Perry's back. Perry gasped and fell to the ground.

I had a feeling Perry was just playing dead, and I was right. Once Chuck went to enter Perry's tent, Perry rose quickly, took his rusty blade and started stalking Chuck. I felt so useless, but in a moment of enlightenment, I grabbed my walkie talkie and turned on the static. The noise made Chuck turn around at just the right moment as Perry slammed into him; I watched as they wrestled on the ground. Perry may have had a weight advantage, but he was injured. Still, Perry drew his rusty blade and jammed it into Chuck's side. I realized this was my last chance, so I used all my remaining strength to crawl over there. Once I got within reach, I picked up another sharp bone from Perry's tent, but this time I thrust it through Perry's neck. Perry collapsed, but this time he didn't get back up.

Loose Ends

After Perry's death, the entire police department arrived, including FBI agents. Chuck made sure I was immediately attended to by the EMTs. They didn't waste a second of time. I was put on a stretcher and driven to the hospital. It was all over the news, when I arrived, I overheard a tv just outside my room as the nurses and doctors did their best to save what was left of me. There were so many people in the room. I couldn't actually see the TV, but I could hear it. Apparently, Chuck was arrested for not executing proper interviews and background checks on any of his employees. Families of the deceased sued Chuck for every last penny he had.

After they finished talking about Chuck's story, they started investigating Perry's real occupation. Based on what investigators discovered, Perry was raised by his father and at a circus, and his father had also been a clown; however, there was evidence on

Perry's body that he had been physically abused by his father his entire life. Investigators also mentioned how Perry's father was found mutilated in the back of a pick up truck 15 years ago. It was determined that Perry had killed his father since the similarities in causes of death matched most of Perry's victims. I wanted to hear more, but the nurse shut off the TV. I was released from the hospital months later only to be detained and sent to a looney bin after I attempted to kill myself from all the trama I had endured.

There were a lot of people in the looney bin, and lots of them were scared or intimidated as they saw that I was a living victim of the gruesome killings from the Harlem Fair. Since I was stuck there, I read a lot of books. I even behaved, which got me access to a computer once a week. Last week while on the computer, I was curious if anything new had been discovered about Perry. Most of the articles said the same stuff I had heard at the hospital, until I found one about several bodies found in remote areas across the U.S, and how they all died years ago, but they were all killed the same way, Perry's way. It turns out Perry was more than just a clown; his real profession was being a serial killer. So I guess you can call him a killer clown. Hahahahaha!

My Whispering Addiction

My Whispering Addiction Story Summary

What starts as just thoughts in the back of Derek's mind turns into whispers. Derek does his best to ignore the whispers because they are inhuman, but the more he is bullied, the more whispers he hears. When things keep progressively getting worse, it gets to the point where Derek can't help but listen. Once he starts listening, he finally hears an offer he can't refuse. Derek ends up using the whispered suggestions, and they work so well at killing his problems that he develops an addiction for more.

The Whispers

Derek -

It wasn't until my freshman year of high school that I started hearing the whispers. At first, I pretended not to hear them because they were unethical. Eventually, I noticed they became more frequent when I was furious, sad, or depressed. I ignored the whispers for as long as I could; however, it was when Lincoln, the high school bully, poured chocolate milk on my head and shoved me to the ground that I decided to listen.

I lay there with milk dripping down my face, and that's when I heard the whisper that would solve my problem. I couldn't ignore it anymore. I followed the whisper's instructions. I rose from the floor, grabbed a pen from my pocket, and thrust it into Lincoln's neck. Blood spewed everywhere, and I smirked at the fear and pain in his eyes. I couldn't help but smile. Just as quickly as the whisper appeared, it disappeared, and replacing its presence was a sense of power. For the first time since I could remember, I was happy.

Of course I was the one to get into trouble even though I claimed it was self defense. I told the principal how the same kid had bullied me the whole year, and when he shoved me on the ground, I felt threatened and felt the need to defend myself. The principal wasn't buying any of it; he told me that I should've reached out for help if what I claimed was true. I was livid because he said he was going to call my parents, and I was most likely going to be arrested.

Anger and fear cleansed me of any remorse, and along with it came a whisper. I listened to the whisper as it made its suggestion. Its suggestion was cruel, but I was then reminded of how the last whisper got rid of my bully. Then I remembered the power I felt after words. I waited until the principal turned around and grabbed the phone. Then, without hesitation, I grabbed the stapler from his desk and bashed the back of his head with it. I didn't mean to kill him. That was not my intention. He had never wronged me; however, I needed to prevent him from calling the police. The whispers got louder and more horrific. They were so loud I wanted to scream, so I told them to screw off, and just like that, they disappeared.

But once they disappeared, any sense of power I felt flushed away, and I just felt worthless. As I exited the principal's office, Lincoln's friend group found me alone in the hallway. They surrounded me and beat the crap out of me. I thought I was going to die, but as they strangled me, the whispers came back. They reminded me of how powerful they made me feel, and that all I needed to do was listen and my problems would cease to exist. I made my choice. I listened to the gentle breeze that tickled my ear. Moments later I raised my hand and dug my nails into one bastard's arm, causing him to groan in pain.

I quickly rose to my feet. The power began to flow through my veins. I smiled and snapped his neck. One of the others attempted to punch me, but after hearing another whisper, I grabbed his fist, twisting it and causing it to snap. He started to scream, and I watched as the others ran away. I towered over the one with the broken wrist, and he pleaded with me to not hurt him. I smiled as I told him it would only hurt for a second. I grabbed him and dragged him to the bathroom where I drowned him. If anyone saw him, they would just think he was sick. Once again, listening to the whispers made my problems go away, so I promised I would never stop listening. Right then, another whisper reminded me that I needed to take care of the one that ran away.

I darted through the halls searching for him, waiting for a whisper to give me directions. As I waited, I heard the front metal school doors squeak open. I turned around and saw the jerk escaping. I chased him outside where he ran into the road and got hit by a truck. A whisper informed me to flee the scene, so I did. I didn't know where to go, so I walked back home.

As I walked up my driveway, I noticed my Mom's car was there, and her asshole boyfriend's car too. I grabbed my key, unlocked the door, and pushed it open. Seconds after entering, I heard my Mom asking why I was home. She sounded scared, and just as I was about to tell her a lie, I noticed a bruise on her eye and a cut on her chin. I rushed towards her, hugging her and asking what happened. Before she could answer, I heard Tyler's voice boom, "She fell!" I turned around and screamed at him, calling out his bullshit.

Tyler raised his voice at me, demanding that I shut up before he did the same to me. When I told him to go fuck himself, he charged at me, but my mom ran into him and yelled, "Don't you dare touch my son!" He smacked my mom so hard across her face that she slammed into the wall. Tears washed down my face, and my fear was replaced with anger. I went silent as he made his way toward me with a belt. I just stood there and waited, but there was no whisper. Tyler smacked me so hard that my head banged into the countertop. Blood oozed from my head, and I felt disoriented. I questioned where the whispers went when I needed them. I felt abandoned, but this time I didn't wait for a whisper's help. I slowly rose from the floor and sprinted into the kitchen where I searched for the sharpest knife. I quickly found a meat cleaver, and I threw it at Tyler. The cleaver hit him dead center right between his eyes. He fell on the ground, and I felt the power again.

I looked at my mom who was curled in a ball motionless on the floor. I ran to her side and shook her. I didn't get a reaction, so I felt for a pulse and found the slightest one. I cried because I feared my mom was going to die. I grabbed my cell phone and began to dial 911 when a whisper aggressively pierced through my ear, causing me to drop the phone. I started talking to myself out loud, screaming at the whisper for leaving me to face my Mom's abusive boyfriend by myself. The whisper claimed it wasn't my problem; it was my mom's. I argued with the voice, but then it told me it came back to get rid of my problem. I told it my problem was saving my mom.

The whispers replied that they knew and that she was the problem. I cried as the whisper told me I needed to leave and let her die on the floor. I cussed out the voices in my head, but once again, they reminded me of how they were kind and how they got rid of my problems. Then a whisper lingered through the air, reminding me what would happen if I ignored them.

I stood still as I felt the last teardrop dribble down my face. Then I ran into my room and grabbed all the money I had saved over the years. Next, I went into my mom's room and took her money, too. The whisper claimed it would make it look like my mom and her boyfriend had been the victims of a deadly robbery.

I decided to catch a bus since I was tired of walking. I waited until the last stop to get off. It was in the city, which was the perfect place for me to disappear. I walked off the bus and took a look around the city. It was dark and crowded. I walked down a dark alley when I heard a voice telling me to freeze. I turned around, and there was a man in a ski mask with a gun pointed at me. He told me to get on my knees and give him all my money.

I laughed and told him he should turn around and be on his way. The man called me a wise guy, cocked his gun, and put it to my head. I smiled as a whisper danced past my ear. I quickly ducked and grabbed his arm. I bit it and punched him in the face. He dropped his gun, so I picked it up, shoved the nozzle in his mouth, and pulled the trigger. After watching his head explode, I felt the feeling of power again. I loved it.

The sense of power only lasted a few hours, resulting in me feeling like my old pathetic self. I missed the feeling of power I craved. I did my best to resist the urge to go find trouble just so I could hear the whispers and feel the power they gave me. As I was being tempted by my own selfish desire, my stomach rumbled. I was hungry. I looked around for a place where I could get some food and found some shitty looking pizza place, but I was so hungry I didn't care. I walked through the dirty glass door and made my way to the counter. I was looking at what pizza they had out when a customer behind me told me to hurry up.

I turned around and told him he'd better shut his mouth or I would do it for him. As I turned around to order, a crabby looking old man asked me what I wanted. I asked for the last slice of pepperoni pizza, but while I was still ordering, the guy behind me bought the last slice out from under me, cussed me out, and laughed in my face. I barked at the old man for letting someone else order when it was my turn. He claimed he didn't give a shit and said I would have to pick something else.

I couldn't resist anymore. The whisper kept swirling around me pressuring me to listen. The old man asked if I was listening to anything he was saying, and I told him, "Oh, I'm listening all right." I lifted myself onto the counter, climbed over, and got in the man's face as he screamed at me to get out. I told him I had other plans. I took a bread roller and whacked him in the head with it. Then I tied him up and poured sauce and cheese and pepperoni on him. Finally, I shoved him in the oven and set the timer for an hour. I watched in excitement as the sauce burned his skin and the cheese melted on to him. I felt the power surge through me again, so I turned around and left, chuckling on the way out.

It must have been my lucky day because I noticed the jerk who had been behind me in line was waiting for a bus. I walked stealthily behind him and waited until the bus came speeding down to the bus stop. Just as it began to slow down, I shoved him into the street where he was crushed by the massive bus. I thought to myself, *Well, at least he didn't miss the bus*, and I laughed. The sense of power that I felt from earlier magnified into something stronger, and I was happy; however, I realized I needed to flee, as I was involved in what is now a crime scene.

Karma's A Bitch

The feeling of power from back-to-back whispers dissolved the next morning, and when it disappeared, I felt worse than ever before. I was sick. I had a fever, and I felt worthless. I was depressed and desperately craved more power. I rose from the park bench where I had been sleeping and stumbled through the city streets. I felt like the scum at the bottom of someone's shoe as I went around looking for trouble. My intentions were never to cause problems; they were to get rid of my bullies and significant life problems. But things were different now, and I had changed. The lone breeze and dark sky caused me to yawn. So I stumbled back to the park bench and fell into a deep sleep.

I was abruptly awoken from a deep sleep by the sound of someone continuously honking their horn. I slowly sat up and came face to face with a red truck with its windows rolled down blasting music. I smiled, reached into my pocket, pulled out a twenty-dollar bill, and waved it back and forth. I chuckled as I gave the driver a thumbs up. I needed a ride.

One of the passengers stepped out of the truck and asked where I was headed, so I told him the name of a town just outside the city. The man looked at me and laughed, so I pulled out another twenty-dollar bill. His smile faded, and he claimed they could take me there for fifty bucks. I sighed and told him, "You got yourself a deal," and I followed him as he pointed for me to enter the rear passenger seat. When I sat down in the back, the truck sped off. I counted a total of three guys in the truck with me.

I asked them why they were blasting music while circling around the poorer neighborhoods in the area. The guy in the back next to him claimed it was a way of showing dominance, and the guy in the front agreed with him. The driver said they were sending a message. I nodded and told them they sure sent a message all right. It was a long car ride, and I damn well knew these pricks were going to take me out to the middle of nowhere so they could rob me of all my money.

Bingo. Just like that, their car slowed to a stop, and they all turned towards me, demanding I give them everything I had. The guy next to me punched me and pushed me out of the truck. I hit the gravel hard, but I still managed to smile while they all jumped out of the truck. I quickly got to my feet and ran around the truck. I snapped a rusty pipe off of the truck and swung it at one of the guys. The pipe made a cracking sound and the man fell to the ground, his head caved in.

The power began to surge through me again. I started laughing as the jerk in the front charged me. When he was only a few feet away, I stabbed him in the chest with the pipe and tossed him on the ground. The energy I felt was the same as the other day, but I wanted more. I turned to face the driver who pulled out a switchblade, cussing at me while he made his may towards me. He lunged at me, and his blade sliced my arm. I charged at him, knocking us into the bed of his truck.

When I punched him, he cut me again. I was so enraged that I grabbed him by his throat and began choking him until he passed out. Towering over him, I dragged his limp body inside the truck. I positioned him in the passenger seat and closed the seat on him so he wouldn't be able to move. Then I cut the seat belt, wrapped it around his head, and tied it to his speaker. I turned the music to full blast. Finally, I went into the back seats and cut those seat belts as well. I used those to tie the one I stabbed outside to the truck bed.

I hopped into their truck and shifted the gear into reverse, making sure to run over the one lying on the ground. I then shifted it into drive and sped off so the one tied to the truck bed was being dragged on the pavement. I then made sure to turn the bass of the radio to its max and played some death metal. The music was so loud I couldn't hear his screams, but I knew he was screaming all right. I started chuckling because I felt like a hero who would get rid of the scum of the earth.

I made my way to the nearest town with a working gas station and decided to stop. While I was filling up the truck, there was a strong breeze that made my hair flow in the wind. It warned that I needed to get rid of the bodies to prevent any problems. I loosened the restraints on the man next to me and dragged him to the back of the building. I went inside and bought a gas can and some matches. I filled up the gas can and poured it around the two men's bodies.

Before I lit the match, I realized that the worker inside was a witness. I didn't want to hurt him, but I had to listen to the whisper. After running out of gas, I went to the pumps and sprayed gas everywhere. I hopped inside the truck and lit one match, then used it to light the whole box. I rolled down the window, tossing the flaming box, and I hit the gas pedal to the floor. I watched in the rearview mirror as the place ignited into a huge flame, which looked like hell itself.

The power I felt within was unnatural; it was too much. I no longer felt like a hero. I felt like the devil himself. The whispers were so loud that I felt like scum, and I was going almost 150 mph. I looked at myself in the rearview mirror, and I didn't recognize myself. Whoever I saw was evil. So I used whatever remaining soul and morals I had left to stop myself. That's when, on the other side of the road, I saw the first vehicle I had seen all day. It was headed my way, and it was a semi. I told myself I was the problem and ignored the whispers. I turned my wheel and swerved into the semi truck.

An Abominable Christmas Story Summary

It was just another Christmas for Pat and his family, as the snow fluttered down from the sky. Matt had finally turned 18, so when his grandparents came to visit on Christmas Eve, Matt's grandfather warned him of the Bad Man's List and what happened to the kids who ended up on it. Matt's father said it wasn't true, so Matt blew it off as an old folk tale. However, he ended up finding out the hard way the next day.

Christmas Eve

Pat -

The thick fluffy snow whirled down upon the ground. It was just like any other Christmas Eve. My Dad was placing presents under the tree and setting up our stockings while mother made hot cocoa. We had the Christmas music playing, and its cheerful tone echoed throughout the house. Everyone was happy.

My sister and I turned on the TV to watch "The Grinch," but just as we turned up the volume, there was a sturdy knock at the door. My sister went over to open it, and there stood our Grandma. I sprung up from the floor to give her a hug. Then, I looked out the front door and saw Papa making his way to the door with a sack of gifts. I bolted out the door in my socks and gave him the biggest hug. He gave me a pat on the shoulder and asked if I could take the sack.

I grabbed it from him and brought it inside. I put the huge bag next to the tree. My father immediately opened it and placed the gifts under the tree. I heard Papa call out, telling my dad to not take them out. "Why?" my dad asked. "What's going to happen? Will I end up on the naughty list?" While they argued, my mother pulled up a chair so grandma could sit down. I watched as Papa plopped down on the couch. My dad seemed annoyed, until my mother mentioned that the hot cocoa was ready.

My sister brought out a small table, which my mother placed the tray on. We all grabbed a mug and drank. My grandmother started the conversation, asking if we had been good this year. "Of course," my sister replied. Then Pops looked at me, saying, "You're definitely on the naughty list." I laughed and told him there was no such thing. I also knew there was no such thing as Santa. My father gave me a stern look, so I mentioned that I was just joking around.

My grandfather looked at my father, then said, "You're right, kiddo. There's no naughty list, only the Bad Man's List." My dad yelled at him to shut his mouth and said we didn't need to hear that bullshit story he was told as a kid. However, my mother told him to calm down, so Pops continued.

Pops -

When I was a boy, there was a myth or legend or even a story, if you choose to call it that, but it was told to scare us so we would be good, and it worked pretty damn well, at least for most of us. According to the story, if you were a good child, you and your family would be on the good list and safe from the Bad Man's List.

 My son Jordan told me to shut up, but the kids looked interested, and I wanted them to be aware of the dangers of misbehaving. Pat urged me to go on, so I did. I told them what happened to the bad kids in my neighborhood. I told them how on Christmas Eve they were there, but on Christmas morning they were gone. Not only were the bad kids gone, but their families disappeared as well. The only thing left inside their houses was a message on the wall, drawn with blood. The messages would always say: *Thanks for the coal. Merry Christmas!*

However, that wasn't even the worst part. The Bad Man would leave their heads inside their stockings! I told them that it happened every year until I left that town and met their grandmother. Matt started laughing at me, claiming his joke was better. I scolded Pat, telling him it was true and to not ignore the story. Then my son talked over me, saying, "Good one, Dad. Now let's come back to reality and open some presents." I gave him a disappointed look and sipped my hot chocolate. I figured he didn't want them to know that it happened to his best friend.

Pat -

Grandpa told a damn good story all right. If I'm being honest, it creeped me out, so I just started laughing out loud so he would stop talking. I was also offended by the fact Pops said I would be on the naughty list, but my sister wouldn't. Now would be a good time to tell you, if you haven't already figured it out, but my sister is the "perfect" child. You know, the one every parent hopes to have. She volunteers her time, gets straight As in school, she never gets in trouble, and she even has a job.

So what does that make me? Good question. I'm not a bully or jerk to people, but I'm not afraid to get my hands dirty when people get in my face. This causes me to get into dozens of fights. I also like to keep to myself, although at home I don't really do much besides stay in my room. Now the one bad thing you can tie me to is my friend group. Since I get into a lot of fights and stand up for myself, the popular kids at school dislike me because their money doesn't scare me. Therefore, I hang out with people like me who also stand up for themselves. Unfortunately, most of my friends are troubled kids, as they're not like me. Don't get me wrong now. I love my family, especially my Papa, so it really hurt when he told me I would be on the Bad Man's List.

After we finished our hot cocoa, my grandmother asked my sister and me how our senior year of high school was going. After hearing my perfect sister brag about her grades, I got up and went to my room. I was happy for my sister, but being reminded constantly how much better she was than me was depressing.

I slammed my door shut and plopped on my bed. Only a few moments after, I heard knocks on my door. I didn't answer, but the door creaked open, and my Papa entered. He sat on my bed next to me and put his arm around me; he told me how much he loved me. He told me he was just trying to protect me from what happened to my father. I asked what happened, but then my dad walked in and told Grandpa to get out.

He tried to explain himself, but my father wasn't having it, so he grabbed my Papa and pulled him out of my room. I could hear them arguing and shouting down the hall, and then the front door slammed shut. I decided to exit my room to see what was happening. It turned out my dad kicked Pops out. Since Pops wasn't welcomed, my grandmother decided to leave, too, scornfully yelling at my father. I watched as they got into their Jeep and disappeared. My mom started yelling at my father, but he didn't care. He walked up to me and yelled, "Don't listen to a word that old bag says." I was afraid, so I nodded. Then we all went and did our own things. My dad was just watching out the window while I listened to music.

In the middle of my favorite song, I heard my mother shout, "Dinner's ready!" so I took out my earbuds and made my way to the kitchen table. I noticed that it was already pitch black outside. My father was still staring out the window, so I tapped him on the shoulder and told him dinner's ready. My father looked at me with a blank stare, gave me a hug, and together, we went into the kitchen. We all sat down and ate, except for my father.

My dad had his plate full of food but wasn't paying attention to it; he was still staring out the front window from the table. My mom tried starting a conversation, but it quickly faded since my dad never responded. After perhaps the most awkward dinner ever, we all placed our dishes in the sink. My mom gave my father a kiss on the cheek and put his plate in the fridge. Dad finally spoke, saying it was time for bed. My sister and I looked at each other with concern on our faces. I watched as everyone went to their rooms, while my dad made sure all the doors and windows were locked before joining mom.

I closed my bedroom door and got into bed. Once I lay down, I became uncomfortable because the house became freezing cold, so I got up to grab some blankets, then returned to my bed. I was still freezing and did not understand why. I tried to ignore the cold, but I couldn't, and then my cell phone rang. It was Papa. He asked how I was feeling. I told him how, out of nowhere, the house had just become freezing cold. He began speaking loudly, and I could hear the fear in his voice. He told me to stay in my room, and that he was on his way. My phone got so cold it must have frozen. I could no longer hear Pop's voice.

Let Me In

My grandparents didn't live too far away, maybe 15 minutes, so when I heard knocks at the front door, I began to sweat. I opened my bedroom door and went down the hall. I was a few feet from the front door when a voice called my name. It was coming from the other side of the door, I hesitated, and I heard my grandfather's voice asking me to open the door.

I put my hand on the door handle but then remembered my Papa told me to not open the door. I took my hand from the door handle and backed away. The knocks continued, this time louder, but this time I was being ordered to open the door because my Papa claimed he was freezing. I began to cry and stared at the door; the voice began to plead that I open the door. I thought maybe my grandfather flew like a bat out of hell to get here, and maybe it actually was him, and when he tried calling me and I didn't answer, he tried knocking on the door. After realizing this possibility,

I grasped the handle and unlocked the top lock. It made a loud clicking sound.

Just before I unlatched the bottom lock, I heard a door fly open and footsteps sprinting behind me. Then something grabbed me, pulling me away from the door. They put their hand over my mouth, shushing me. It was my dad. The knocks became frantic, the voice on the other side said my dad had locked him out and demanded I let him in. I threw my dad's hand off of me and stared him down. He tried to grab me, but I put my hand on the last lock and threatened to unlatch it. I would've opened the door in that moment if it wasn't for the fear I saw in my father's eyes. He told me to lock the top lock before it was too late.

The door started to shake, the bottom lock snapped, and the door started to creak open. My dad bolted towards me, slamming his body into the door to force it shut. He yelled for me to lock the top lock, so I did. The pounding on the door was aggressive, and the door started to crack. My father told me to run and to find Papa. When I questioned him, he told me that it was not Papa at the door; it was the Bad Man. He started to sob and said he was just trying to protect me.

The door flung open, launching my dad into the wall. What I saw walking into the room was traumatizing. It was a freakishly thin figure covered in thick white fur. It had long sharp nails and yellow fangs. Screaming this time, my father told me to run! I raced to my room, and down the hall, I could hear my father let out what sounded like a battle cry. I entered my room and noticed my window was frozen shut. I heard stomping behind me. I saw my father covered in blood, swinging a knife at the beast. My father yelled for me to smash my window and get to Grandpa's. I frantically looked around, trying to figure out what to use. I tried a bunch of random items, smashing them into my window just to have them shatter into pieces. I turned around to see what else I could grab, and right before my eyes I watched the creature grasp my father's head. It twisted its hands, and I could hear the bones breaking. Then the creature growled and ripped my father's head from his neck. I watched as he used the blood spewing from his body to paint all over the walls. After he was done smearing blood on the wall, he shoved my father's head in a stocking and started to pace towards me. Tears flowed down my face like a river. I used all of my emotions, turning them into rage and punched my window. My fist shattered the glass, but I got cuts all over it. I didn't care. I needed to escape, so I jumped out my bedroom window.

I landed hard on my shoulder, but thankfully there was enough snow to cushion my impact with the ground. I stumbled to my feet and began to make my way to the road. There was so much snow that I couldn't really see the road, but I could still see the house. When I looked back at the house, I saw the

Bad Man climb out my window, and he had two more stockings. He felt my gaze, turned so he was facing me, and he opened the stockings revealing my mother's and sister's heads. I screamed and trudged through the snow, trying to get away. I could hear the sound of snow crunching behind me; he was closing in. That's when I saw a dim light and the sound of a vehicle. I realized it must have been a car, so I lunged for the road. The pavement was frozen, and when I landed, I heard a crunch. I had broken my left leg. I turned to see the creature just a few yards away from me.

I used any strength I had left and scooted myself to the other side of the road. The creature stepped into the road, and he must not have seen the lights because a truck smashed into him. The beast was sent flying into the snow bank, and the truck's bumper was totaled. Then the driver got out and made his way towards me. When the figure was only a few feet away, I recognized him: Grandpa! He saw my tears. I started to cry and mumble, and he picked me up off the ground and helped me into his truck.

He hopped into the driver seat and stepped on the gas. He looked at me and said, "Hang in there, son. It's not over." We drove to his and grandma's house. He jumped out of the car and opened my door, helping me out. He said we needed to get inside before the Bad Man found me. I asked my Papa what the fuck was going on and watched as he did the same thing as my father, checking to make sure everything was locked. After barricading the front door, he took a seat on the couch and looked at me. I could see the pain in his eyes as he carefully chose his words. He took a deep breath before telling me why this was actually happening.

My grandpa reminded me of the story earlier about the Bad Man's List, and the reason he told me was not to scare me but to protect me. He continued, saying how the creature had affected both him and my father when they both were 18. For my Papa, he lost his girlfriend at the time, and as for my father, he lost his best friend. It was scary, but it still didn't add up. I asked why the Bad Man was coming after me. Pop told me the reason was because I had no real friends or anyone I cared about besides my family, so that was its way of punishing me. I asked him why dad denied the story. My grandpa guessed that my dad hoped if I never heard the story, it wouldn't happen to me.

I asked if that was true, but before he could answer, I felt a gaze from outside the house, and the room began to freeze, this time more quickly. My Papa got up and hobbled into the kitchen. He came back with a bundle of wood, tossing it into the fireplace. As he lit the fire, I grabbed a bunch of candles and began lighting them all near the door and windows to keep them from freezing. Pop directed me to stand by the fireplace while he went and grabbed an ax. We heard the voice again; this time it was grandma's. She yelled that we needed to open the door as she was in danger. My papa looked at me, telling me if we made it until the morning we would be safe. The Bad Man only has Christmas day to hunt the ones on his list, and he can never repeat.

The candle flames began to shrink, so my Grandpa tossed more wood into the fireplace to make up for the lack of heat. Sadly, it wasn't enough. The door had nearly frozen over and began to crack and shake. The lock shattered off the door, and it swung open as the bastard walked through. The man was no longer thin, he was fat, and he moved slowly. My Papa yelled at him to get back, but it shuffled forward. It grinned as it put its freakishly large hands around my Papa's neck and strangled him. I witnessed the beast strangle my grandfather to death.

Once my grandpa's face turned purple, the creature grasped his head and twisted. It bellowed as it wrenched my Papa's head from his body. As blood splattered everywhere, the creature stared at me while forming a bloody smile. It began to tear my papa's arms from his dead body. I couldn't watch. I had seen enough. Crying, I turned around and ran to the kitchen. I reached into the cupboard, taking out some cooking oil. I poured the entire bottle all around the kitchen. I looked back at the Bad Man jamming a hook into the severed head.

I waited until the thing looked up at me, and with one motion I lit a match and tossed it on the ground. Fire raged through the house, causing everything to thaw. The fire got out of control fast; it engulfed the house with us inside. The beast began to roar, and it forced its way outside. I followed him outside and watched him disappear into the blizzard. Just a few moments later, I heard the sirens. Figures in yellow suits were screaming, and one of them helped me away from the house. I turned my head to my left and saw the fire trucks. While the firefighters battled the flames, I was questioned by police. I told them everything, but I don't think they believed me. They just asked if I had any other family I could stay with.

Years later

It's been 20 years since the nightmare, but here again the snow fluttered. It was Christmas Eve, and my family gathered by the Christmas tree. However, it wasn't until my 18-year-old son grasped my hand and told me to stop staring out the window that I joined my family. I decided to not tell my son about the old story. I hoped if I didn't tell him he would be safe, and I thought he was, that was until I was awoken to a loud pounding on the front door. Before I could get up, I heard my son's footsteps approach the door. I rushed to my bedroom door, pushing it open, but I was too late. I watched my son unlock the door, and the door creaked open as the Bad Man pushed on it with a grin on his face!

My Dangerous Admirer

My Dangerous Admirer
Story Summary

What starts off as just another fight with her husband takes a violent turn, and Tara decides she wants out of her marriage, which opens the door for someone else to fill that position. However, sometimes it's hard to find someone to replace your ex, which may make it easier for them to replace you.

The Last Straw

Tara -

It was Friday night, and the rain was pounding on the kitchen windows. My husband was screaming at me about the house being a mess. When I tried to defend myself, he slapped me and called me a bunch of foul names. That's when I lost my temper, and I punched him square in the face. I'm used to getting into screaming matches with him, but he has never put his hands on me. I pushed him out of my way and stomped up the stairs.

I could hear him follow me upstairs; he was screaming at me and asked what I thought I was doing. I told him I was grabbing my stuff, and I would see myself out. He put his hand on my shoulder, but I smacked it off. He looked as if he were going to cry. As I made my way downstairs to the kitchen, I could hear him pleading with me to stay. He claimed he just had a bad day and a few too many beers.

I stared at him, looking him up and down, and I questioned why I had not already walked out the door. I reached for my coat and car keys. Then Alex grabbed my arm and told me I wasn't going anywhere.

I used my key and jabbed it into his arm. He screamed in pain, and called me a bitch! I used that moment to grab a picture from our wedding, and I bashed it over his head. He fell to the floor, causing a loud thud. While he lay unconscious, I yanked my keys from his arm and walked out to my car. I got inside and drove to a friend's house.

Moving on

I pulled into Bella's driveway, and with my arms full of my belongings, I approached the front door. I used my knuckle to press the doorbell since my hands were full. I waited patiently until the door opened. I was confused when a younger looking guy opened the door. I hesitantly asked if Bella was here, and I heard her voice from upstairs telling me to come in. I walked in, and Bella came thumping down the stairs, her hair bouncing with each step.

When she saw me with all my things, she panicked, ran towards me, and gave me a hug. She introduced the young man as her boyfriend, Stan. She asked Stan to take my things and bring them to the guest room. I tried to tell him it was fine, that I could handle it, but Stan insisted. So I sat down and had a talk with Bella about what happened. I waited until her boyfriend went outside to get the rest of my things before I began to tell her everything. When she heard me say Alex hit me, she gasped, and I saw both rage and sympathy glow in her eyes. She told me that I was welcome to stay as long as I needed. I told Bella how she was the best and how grateful I was that she was in my life.

After about ten minutes of Stan going in and out to unload my car, he suggested we all go see a movie. Bella was hesitant and glanced for my approval before answering. I nodded because I actually thought it was a good idea. Stan said he would drive, so we grabbed our wallets and phones, and we hopped into Stan's truck. Bella sat in the back with me to make sure I was okay. I told her I was fine, which was a lie, but I acted as if I actually was fine.

Stan parked close to the front doors, and we got out and made our way to the theater. Once we made it inside, we asked the person in the booth what movies were playing. We ended up choosing a comedy with some famous actors in it. After we paid and got our tickets, Bella and Stan decided they would reserve our seats while I waited in the snack line. There weren't many people there, but the few in front of me were ordering the whole snack bar! Finally, it was my turn, so I ordered a large popcorn with melted butter and three large sodas. The total came to around $40, so I pulled out my wallet and grabbed my debit card.

Just as I was reaching to pay the cashier, I heard someone call my name. I turned to see a well-dressed man that I had never seen before jogging towards me. He cut in front of me, and handed the cashier his credit card. I thanked him and told him it wasn't necessary, but he insisted. When I asked him why he paid for me, he admitted he just thought I was cute, and he hoped he could make my day. He asked if he could join me for the movie. I said sure, and we walked into the theater. I asked him how he knew my name. He replied that he heard one of the people I was with say my name. I thought that was cute and saw no trouble with it. He asked what movie we were seeing. I told him it was a comedy.

He reached out for my hand, holding it firmly as we walked past the rows. I spotted my friends in the back; they were sitting in the middle of the row. When Bella saw me, she gave me a curious look, wondering why I had a random guy join us. I told her about how he paid for all of our snacks and called me cute. She nodded and reached out her hand, introducing herself. The man returned her handshake, saying, "It's nice to meet you, Bella, I'm Johnny." After the movie, I turned Johnny down when he asked for my number. Suddenly, the nice guy was gone. I could see the steam flow from his ears; he was livid. He got in my face, and called me a bitch.

Bella must have seen it because she called for Stan. Moments later, Stan shoved Johnny to the ground, where he towered over him, telling him to beat it. The nicely dressed man got up and brushed the dirt off his shirt. He gave me a glare and disappeared in the distance. Bella broke the silence and asked what the hell that guy's problem was. I shrugged my shoulders and mentioned that I rejected him when he asked for my number. Bella shouted, "What a freak!" Stan was still looking off into the distance, making sure the man was gone.

After a few long moments, Stan turned around and said we needed to leave. The car ride back was completely silent. When we finally got back to their house, we all washed up and got ready for bed. Stan wished me a goodnight while Bella went to retrieve some extra pillows.

I was sitting there alone in the room when my phone buzzed. I reached for my phone, but I was interrupted by Bella kicking open the door with an arm full of pillows and blankets. She told me to not let that creep from earlier keep me up, and she placed everything on my bed and hugged me, wishing me a goodnight.

I waited until the door closed before I got off the bed to use the bathroom. As I made my way to the bathroom, my phone buzzed again. I gingerly walked towards the bed and grabbed my phone. I had three new messages, one missed call, and one new voicemail.

I looked at the texts; one was from my husband. It was an apology text, and it was a few pages long. He claimed that he was just an idiot, and how he loved me and wanted me back. I decided not to answer, so I left him unread. I checked out the other two messages. It was strange that they were both from the same unknown number. The first message claimed that I was a horrible person, and the second one was a threat about how he would find me and punish me. I was already freaked out, so when the same number called my phone again, I shrieked and dropped my phone on the ground. I waited until it stopped ringing.

Finally, I picked it up; in a state of panic, I went to my mailbox and listened to the new message I had just received. The voicemail started off quiet but quickly grew louder. It sounded like metal scraping metal; then a male voice boomed, "Watch your back, bitch!" I smashed my phone on the ground and sat on the floor and began to cry. I ended up crying myself to sleep.

The Next Morning

I woke up to the sound of someone knocking on the bedroom door. The door creaked open, and I heard Bella's voice announce Stan was making breakfast, and if I wanted any to come get some. I mumbled I would be there in a minute. I needed to change my clothes because I was drenched with sweat. I stumbled towards my duffle bag full of my clothes. Before I changed, I decided it would be a good idea to shower first. I grabbed a change of clothes and made my way to the bathroom, closing the door behind me.

Bella must have heard the door shut, because she hollered up the stairs, asking if I was joining them. I answered that I was just going to take a quick shower, so she asked me if she should get a plate out for me. I shouted, "Yes, please!" and I waited to see if she would respond before I shut the bathroom door again.

I stripped off my sweaty clothes, and I stepped into the shower, pulling the curtain aside. I took my other hand, placed it on the hot water handle, and turned it up all the way. The water came out of the shower head steaming; it burned my skin, but I didn't mind. I always take hot showers. After I finished showering, I turned off the water, exited the shower, and wrapped myself in a towel. While I dried myself off, I couldn't help but glance out the tiny bathroom window. I noticed a black pickup truck parked behind my car that was not there last night. My anxiety took over, so I quickly changed and made my way down the stairs to the kitchen.

Before my foot even had hit the bottom step, I was greeted with a good morning from Stan. He asked how I slept; I lied and told him fine. He pointed to the kitchen, informing me my plate was on the counter. I forced a smile, thanked him, and went to grab my plate. When I turned around, I saw Bella exit the downstairs bathroom.

She must have seen me because she said I was more than welcome to eat in the living room with them. I smiled and followed her down the narrow hallway. Once we got to the living room, I noticed Stan sitting at what looked like a desk. He was on the phone with someone, talking about something related to work. Bella looked at me and flashed me a smile. I smiled back and sat down on the couch.

The food was amazing: bacon with eggs and hashbrowns. I was completely shocked that Bella's boyfriend could cook so well. My husband could never cook like this. I was always the chef. After I was done eating, I returned my plate to the sink, and I heard crackling and rumbling from outside. I figured it must have been lightning, but I decided to look out their kitchen window. I could see the wind whipping through the trees. I looked back at my car as the raindrops splashed my windshield. Then I saw a flash from behind my car. When I turned to see what the flash was from, to my horror I saw the black truck parked directly behind my car with its windshield wipers going crazy. I stared at the truck and noticed another flash; it seemed like someone inside was taking pictures of my car! I screamed, and I immediately heard footsteps pounding on the floor.

Bella shouted, "What's wrong?" I couldn't speak. My hand trembled as I pointed out the window. Bella looked out and shouted, What the fuck!?" Bella called to Stan, and he came jogging down the hallway. He put his hand on Bella's shoulder, and before he could ask what was wrong, she, too, pointed outside. I watched as Stan squinted out the window while Bella made her way to me. She gave me a hug, and I started crying. She told me to calm down and tell her what was going on.

I took a deep breath and started mumbling about the texts I had gotten last night and the voicemail that I received. I told her how someone in that truck was taking pictures of my car. Bella hugged me, trying to get me to relax, and Stan told me to bring him my phone. Bella decided to accompany me back up the stairs into the bedroom. She pushed open the door, and I entered to grab my phone. When I picked it up, I saw that I had over ten new messages, more missed calls, and another voicemail. I was shaking, but I told myself to open the messages. The first text I saw was an image of me. I shrieked and threw my phone at the wall. Then I realized that I never really got a good look at the photo, so I couldn't help but want to see the image again. When I got up and retrieved my phone, I noticed the picture was me getting out of the shower!

I began to sob. I leaned against the wall, sliding down to the floor. Bella ran towards me, gave me another hug, and asked me what I saw. With tears streaming down my face, I told her to take a look herself. She left my side and grabbed my phone. When she opened it, she screamed, and that was when Stan came thumping up the stairs and burst into the room. His face was drenched with sweat, and he glanced at me on the floor crying. Then he turned his attention to Bella, who was frozen in place. He walked over toward her and grabbed the phone from her hand. I watched him as he scrolled through the messages.

Stan paused and yelled, "What the fuck!?" He looked at me, assuring me he would handle the situation. He gently placed my phone on the bed, and I watched him grab a baseball bat from the closet. Bella saw her boyfriend grab the bat, so she ran after him, telling him to not go outside.

I used my remaining strength to crawl towards the bed. I reached for my phone, and I opened it. There were more pictures of me: at work, at my home, and out in public. Tears began to flow down my face like a river, but something told me I needed to listen to the voicemail. I tapped on the new voicemail and pressed play. Just like the last one, it started off quietly, and then I heard the metal sound again.

Finally a voice spoke; it informed me that he had found me and I wasn't safe in that house. I wasn't even done processing what I had just heard when my phone began to ring. Without thinking, I answered it. The same voice from the voicemail spoke, telling me it was a good thing I answered. I screamed at the voice, saying the most despicable things I had ever said in my life. I was interrupted by the voice telling me I had better get my friends to go back inside. Before I could respond, I heard what sounded like a gun being cocked back, and then the call ended.

Not even a second after the call ended, I ran like a bat out of hell down the stairs. I got to the front door just in time to see Stan lift the bat and smash the truck's windshield. The glass shattered, and when Stan lifted the bat to swing it again screaming at the man in the truck, there was a loud bang, and Stan's body collapsed. The truck door opened, and the nicely dressed man stepped out, holding a pistol in his hand. I watched in horror as he walked over to Stan, and stood over him. I could see Stan struggle to get back up. The man watched Stan struggle and then put a bullet through his head.

Bella screamed, and the man turned towards her. I watched as he unloaded three bullets into her chest. I was scared shitless, but when I saw the man face me with a smile on his face, I shrieked and slammed the door shut. I locked both locks on the door and made my way to the back. When I got to the back patio door, I froze, wondering why the man had not forced his way through the front door. Startled by tapping on the glass door behind me, I turned to face the nicely dressed man standing in the back yard with his gun pointed at me.

I screamed and ran to the front door. I heard the glass shatter behind me and the man's footsteps sprinting after me. I quickly unlocked the door and slammed it shut. It must have hit him in the face as I heard him swear out loud. I made sure not to waste any time as I made my way to my car, unlocking it. I hopped inside, put my keys in the ignition, and turned them. The car roared to life, and I shifted into drive. I hit my pedal to the floor, and went right through the fence that separated Bella's house from her neighbors. I raced back to my house. Once I got there, I was relieved to see my husband's truck still in our driveway.

I slammed on the brakes and ran frantically to the front door. I tried opening the door, but it was locked. I couldn't find my key, so I started banging on the door. A few moments later the door swung open, and I fell inside. I looked up to see my husband with a surprised look on his face. I got up off the ground and entered the house, slamming the door behind me. I made sure to lock the door, and I ran into my husband's arms. I told him that I was sorry, and I forgave him for everything. He gave me a big hug and asked why I just stormed inside like that.

I started to tell him about the well-dressed man when I saw the glare of headlights flash through our living room window. I screamed and jumped into my husband's arms, begging him to protect me. He gently placed me on the couch and took a look out the window before disappearing into our bedroom. I could hear him making a mess, throwing things around, and I could tell he was looking for something.

Just as I began to believe everything would be all right, a bullet shot through the front door and pierced the TV that was just a few feet away from me. I screamed as the lock blew off the door and it swung open. I saw the man enter with his pistol pointed at me. He told me again how I was an ungrateful bitch and cocked his gun back. I closed my eyes and prepared to die. I crunched up into a ball and heard a single gunshot. A few seconds later, I opened my eyes to see why I had not been shot. There was blood spewing from the nicely dressed man who lay motionless in our living room. I sniffled and looked to my left where my husband stood with his hunting rifle in his hands. I started to hyperventilate and ran towards my husband, hugging him as hard as I could while my tears soaked his shirt.

He patted me on the back and told me that he hoped I learned my lesson. I stopped crying as I processed what he had just said. I looked up into my husband's face; he had a blank expression as he looked me in the eye. I watched as one single tear drop fell down his face while he put his hands around my neck. My husband threw me on the ground, crawled on top of me, and began to choke me. I could see the rage in his eyes turn into tears as he told me I should've never left him. I tried to fight back, but he overpowered me, and before everything went black, I heard him say I was the one that needed to be replaced.

Consequences

Alex -

I watched my wife as her eyes shut and she took her last breath. I dragged her body into the kitchen where I dismembered it and disposed of it. I won't lie; it was fun hiring a hitman to scare the crap out of her, and even though I paid him to kill her, I couldn't let him have the best part. No, I was the one that needed to kill her. Just like my first wife, she was scum that needed to be replaced. I had to kill the hitman, too, because I couldn't leave any loose ends. After it was all dealt with, I downloaded a dating app and began talking to other girls. I found this one girl whose name was Amber; she said she would be more than happy to go out with me. So I called and made a reservation at a fancy restaurant. A wide grin formed on my face. I hoped she wouldn't leave me or try to replace me like my ex wife did. If she did, she would have to suffer the same fate.
family, thpsychiatrist who promises he will make his

The Shadow Man Story Summary

It hides in the shadows and waits for the perfect moment to strike. Then it tortures a family by abducting their older son. After his disappearance, it appears in the younger brother's dreams every night for three years, causing the family to unravel. In a desperate attempt to save what's left of their family, the father decides to take his son to a psychiatrist who promises he will make his son's nightmares go away.

First Impression

Miguel -

Every night its red eyes glow at me from outside my window, followed by it tapping on my window with its long claws. It's not until I see its jagged teeth form a smile that I wake up from the nightmare drenched in sweat. I have had this same exact nightmare every night since my brother's disappearance three years ago.

My brother Matt was only ten years old the night he disappeared. Only a week after his tenth birthday, I can recall my brother telling my parents about a scary man being in his room at night. Of course, my parents assured him it was just his imagination, but when Matt still refused to sleep alone in his room, my dad finally gave in and took a look around. I watched as my father skimmed over my brother's room, but he paused when he saw what looked like scratches on my brother's window.

He put his hand on the glass and cursed as he cut his hand. He exited the room and stopped in the bathroom where I heard him clean out his cut. I waited outside the bathroom until my father came out. The bathroom door swung open, hitting me in the face. My father saw me on the ground with my nose bleeding and yelled at me for standing behind the door. His rage quickly turned into concern because I started to cry and said I was scared. He picked me up, and we joined my mother and brother in the kitchen. My father put me down and assured Matt there was nothing in his room. My mother interrupted since she could feel the tension between us, and she asked if we wanted ice cream. "Yay!" Matt cheered. Ice cream was his favorite thing in the whole world. I smiled as we left the house and made our way to the car.

I remember hearing a faint whisper that tickled my ear, which caused me to turn back to the house where I saw a figure standing in my brother's room. I watched as it traced the scratch my father cut his hand on with its long nails. The figure then smiled, revealing yellow jagged teeth. Just before I could scream, it held up one finger to its mouth, telling me to be quiet. I looked in fear at the figure as it pointed to my brother who was next to me.

I cocked my head towards my brother to see him entering the car. When I looked back at the window, the figure was gone. In a state of panic, I ran towards the car only to trip over a tree root. I moaned in pain since I had a small cut on my leg. The blood trickled down my leg, and my father opened the car door to see if I was ok. He saw the cut on my leg and poured some water from his water bottle on it. I yelled because the water caused a burning sensation. I did my best to hold back the tears, as my father picked me up and placed me in the back seat next to my brother.

Once we arrived at the ice cream shop, my mother suggested we go to the bathroom before ordering, so my brother walked me to the bathroom where he went inside the stall, locking the door behind him. I waited a minute before asking my brother about what the man he saw at night looked like. There was a short pause before he began describing exactly what I saw at his window. I gulped and asked if the man ever said anything to him.

My brother stuttered, "It tells me that it's going to get me." This spooked me, but I told myself I needed to know more, so I pushed Matt to tell me everything. Matt continued on about how each night since his tenth birthday, the creature would scratch his window, causing it to slowly crack. Each night it would scratch harder and longer, until the sound got so loud he would wake up from his slumber. There was an awkward silence before my brother asked me to drop it. He just wanted to enjoy some ice cream.

After we ate, we ran a few errands before returning home. My father was mostly silent on the way home. My mother tried starting a conversation, but each time, it was just her talking to herself. We finally arrived home, and while my father parked the car, he told us to help mom bring in the groceries. Since Matt was a few years older than I was, he took most of the bags so I didn't have to.

Our mother had handed me the keys, so I could open the door for my brother, but when I put the keys into the door, it creaked open. I told my mother, and she immediately called for my father, demanding he make sure the house was safe.

My dad grabbed our welcome sign off the door to use it as a weapon as he entered. After a few minutes, our dad returned claiming nothing was missing, and there was no one inside. My mother looked around and informed us she must have forgotten to lock the door when we left.

My father took the bags from our mother, and motioned us to follow him inside, so we did. For dinner that night we had pizza, and just between me and my brother, we ate half the pie. After dinner, we all watched a movie together. It was some comedy, which I found boring. So to get away, I said I was going to use the bathroom. On my way to the bathroom, I heard a faint noise from upstairs, and being the curious little boy I was, I decided to investigate. The noise sounded like an animal scratching against the wall, and it was coming from my brother's room. I peered my head around into my brother's room and saw a freakishly tall skinny figure trying to crawl under Matt's bed. Its long nails were scratching his wooden bed frame. It looked as if the creature was trying to pull itself under the bed, but it couldn't fit.

I stared at the thing while breathing heavily. I must have been breathing too loudly because the figure stopped and pushed itself out from under the bed. It stood up, banging its head on the ceiling, and it turned around. Then, with a grin on its face, it attempted to snatch me. However, I was too quick. I let out a gut wrenching scream – it was so loud the thing put its claws over its ears – and I retreated to my brother's closet while my parents came trampling up the stairs.

My mother scooped me up in her arms while my father ran with a knife into my brother's room. My dad looked around and saw nothing. He looked at my mother before suggesting it was bedtime and that maybe tomorrow would be a better day. I attempted to interrupt him, but my mom shushed me and cradled me until I became very sleepy. I can remember her whispering goodnight to me before turning off my bedroom light and closing the door.

I remember the next morning like it was yesterday. I remember waking to my mother's screams. I jumped out of bed and raced to my door, pushing it open. I was met by my father who was crying. He picked me up, hugging me tight. My mom was curled up in a ball sobbing. My father placed me on the ground, then he pulled out his cellphone and made a call. Minutes later, the police arrived.

Unraveling

That horrific morning was three years ago, but it feels like it was only yesterday. Every night since that day, I have had these nightmares about that creature, outside my window trying to get in, and I fear it will come for me next. I will say that every night it progressively gets worse. It always starts off the same way. I hear a whisper, and I ignore it, so it begins tapping on my window. Then I always glance at my window to see the figure perched on my window sill. Once he notices my gaze, he grins and starts scratching at my window like it's a cat post. So how exactly does it get worse?

Well, after each time the figure scratches, the glass cracks, but it never breaks through. But more of the glass cracks every night. I fear the night the window breaks will be the night he comes for me. If that isn't bad enough, while it scratches vigorously, my closet door will squeak open, and I'll see the body of what once was my brother. At this point of the dream, I wake up screaming, drenched in sweat.

For the first few months, my parents would rush to check on me since I would be screaming bloody murder. I would tell them my dreams, and my mother would scream at me that I was sick – that I found it amusing to torture her like this. My father, on the other hand, always walked towards my closet and would check it. He would then pat me on the head and tell me he missed Matt, too.

Eventually, when the dreams didn't stop, my father thought they should take me to see a psychiatrist. I went to see one who stared at me with a very concerned look on his face, and he asked my parents to leave the room so he could talk to me alone. At the time I was scared out of my mind, but I knew it would be better if they left, therefore they wouldn't have to relive the moment of my brother's disappearance.

The doctor pulled up a chair and suggested I take a seat. He told me to relax and asked if I wanted anything to eat or drink. When I shook my head no, he leaned back, crossed his legs, and asked me to tell him my dreams – and to be as descriptive as possible. I was hesitant to answer, and he must have been able to tell. He interrupted, claiming he would not judge me. He told me how the mind has its own ways of coping with tragedies, and that to diagnose if that was the case, I needed to be as descriptive as possible.

I started to shake; my anxiety was through the roof, but I nodded and began to tell him about the same dream I had every night. I studied his face to see how he reacted to my words, but he didn't. This made me more comfortable because I felt he was not judging me.

He waited until after I was done talking to comment. He cracked his knuckles, making a bone-breaking sound. I squirmed, and he lifted his hand, telling me to relax. He said based on my dream, he would guess I must have seen this creature before it took my brother.

Before I answered, I realized that I had never told him that it took my brother, that I only told him my dream. He must have realized I made the connection because he quickly added that my parents had mentioned my brother's disappearance. There was an awkward silence before he spoke again. He sat up straight and cracked his back, making another gross sound. He told me that based on the information I had given him, that this recurring dream was a result of my body not being able to cope with the loss of my brother.

He informed me he was going to prescribe some anxiety medication and some sleeping pills meant for children. I asked if we were done, and the doctor responded by opening his office door. He told me to have a good day, and that he would see me later. I froze and noticed his smile, which revealed some ugly looking yellow teeth.

I honestly found the doctor really creepy, but I told myself he was helping me. I was escorted back to the waiting area where my parents sat, looking stiff as boards. My mother asked the nurse, "How did it go? Is he okay? What is his diagnosis?" The nurse simply told my mother she could ask her questions at the front desk. My mother frowned but followed my father to the front desk. My mom once again asked her questions only to be ignored again; the lady interrupted her, telling her that Dr. Manson would be prescribing some medications for me. My mom argued, demanding that her questions be answered. I watched as my dad had to grab my mom and walk her out of the room.

My father normally would've taken my mom's side and would help her get her answers, but ever since Matt disappeared she'd been a complete mess, and she had lost part of her sanity. My father was sick and tired of her actions; she couldn't move on from Matt's disappearance while he had. However, he was determined to stay and try his best to keep what was left of this family together.

We left the doctor's office, and my father decided to drop me and mom off at home while he went to get my scripts. I watched out the front window as my father drove down the cement road. Once he was out of sight, I felt a tear drop squirm down my face;

being home alone with mom was another nightmare.

I decided to go to my room and wait there until my father returned home. I figured it would be best to avoid mom as much as possible. I evaluated my day, trying to gather any positives from it. Just as I began to feel better, I heard my mom call my name. Any positive energy I had flushed out of me as she called me downstairs again, this time louder.

She was sitting on our living room floor and patted the carpet next to her, telling me to take a seat. She apologized for how she'd been acting lately; then she asked me how my talk with the doctor went. In shock at my mother's new positive attitude, I told her that I found it beneficial. She asked if I would like to continue seeing him. I thought for a moment and replied with a head nod. After we talked, I heard my father's keys begin unlocking the door.

He entered with a drowsy look on his face and said, "Hey, kiddo," as he walked by me. My mother approached him, giving him a hug and taking the bag from him. Then she read the labels and screamed at my father for getting me sleeping pills. My father questioned her and took the bottle from her. After reading the label, he swore to my mom that's what was prescribed. My mother slapped my father, calling him a liar. She started screaming that it was all his fault that Mattew disappeared. I could see tears bubble from my father's eyes as he called her a crazy bitch and shoved her into the wall. He turned towards me, reaching for my hand, telling me we needed to go.

He was only a few inches from grasping my hand when he grunted in pain. My mother was on his back stabbing him repeatedly with a kitchen knife, screaming it was all his fault. My father collapsed and told me to go to my room and lock the door, but I didn't listen because I was too afraid to move. My father used his remaining energy to take out his phone and attempt to call the police; however, my mom slashed his forearm with the blade, causing him to drop the phone.

I saw my father struggle. He looked at me with tears streaming down his face and told me he loved me. After that, my father's head banged on the floor; that's when I realized he was dead, and out of fear of what would happen next, I lunged for my dad's phone and dashed up the stairs to my room. I slammed the door behind me, locking it, but then I remembered my mom had a key, so I pushed anything and everything I could move to barricade myself in.

I opened my dad's phone and called 911. My mother started furiously banging on my door. She was sobbing but simultaneously yelling at me to let her in. Finally, I heard an operator's voice on the phone. I started ranting that my mom had just killed my father and was trying to kill me. I told them I had locked myself in my room but that my mom was forcing her way in. The operator told me to stay calm and asked for my address. I gave it to her, and I stayed on the phone while they sent officers to my house. I watched out my window as eight cop cars parked around the house. I heard them bust down the front door and trample up the stairs. That's when I heard it, the loud voices demanding my mom to drop the knife, my mother screaming in retaliation. She must have charged at them because gunshots flared in response to my mother's screams.

There was pounding on the door, and the officers asked if I was ok. They heard my cries, so they burst through the door and found me sniffling, curled up into a ball. I was comforted by a female officer as she escorted me outside to a squad car. Once inside, they asked me what happened. I told them everything, and once I mentioned my doctor's visit, they interrupted me, asking if I needed to go and talk to him. I remember sniffling and nodding my head.

Dream Free

I watched as the flashing lights danced with one another while the officers drove me back to Doctor Manson's office. Once we arrived, they escorted me in, and they even waited in the waiting room until I was seen.

The same nurse from before walked me to a new room. She told me to take a seat, that the doctor would be right with me. I waited patiently, twiddling my thumbs when the door flung open. It was the doctor; he had a very concerned look on his face as he closed the door behind him. He carried a note pad with him and sat down across from me. He looked at me sadly, apologizing for what had happened to me, and he asked me to tell him exactly what happened, detail for detail. So I did, but as I told him what happened, he slowly began to smirk. After I was done talking, he nodded his head, telling me that he was glad I was still alive, and I thanked him. The doctor then reassured me that I wouldn't have to worry about having the nightmares anymore. I smiled, gullible, asking him how he knew.

He grinned and said only the living can dream. My smile faded as I stared at him. I watched as he stood up, grunted, and began cracking every bone in his body, which made gross popping sounds. I then watched as he reached at the top of his head and began to pull down a zipper. He pulled the zipper down to his waist and stepped out of the human suit he'd been wearing.

I pissed my pants as I realized it was him the whole time. I attempted to scream, but he covered my mouth with his claws. He used his free claw to swipe at the light fixture, causing it to go out. I felt his nails glide along my throat as we disappeared into the darkness.

The Flickering Lamp Post Story Summary

What just starts off as just a high school graduation party slowly turns into a massacre, as teens smoke and drink all night long, to the point where one takes his anger out on an object that is beloved by a dangerous being. Nate and his friends quickly find themselves in a deadly situation where they will be lucky if anyone makes it out alive.

Graduation Night

Nick -

The music was booming, the pretty girls were dancing, and everyone was either wasted or high out of their minds. Now before you start judging us, I would like to inform you that for everyone at this party, it was one of the biggest – if not the biggest – moment in their lives. Graduation is the celebration of what we have accomplished, and once this party was over, we would all have to take the next big step into our lives: college.

But enough talk about college, it's time to party! So if you'll excuse me, it's time for me to go on out with my boys for some beer pong! Yeah, yeah. I know. We're underage. Well, I hate to break it to you, but we don't give a shit! Besides, what's the worst that could happen?

Nate -

I was in the middle of a very intense game of spin the bottle when I noticed my man Nick walking with a bunch of chicks. It looked like they were heading to the bear pong table. I smirked and watched him as he tried impressing the ladies. There was a sudden yelling sound. I turned back to the circle and noticed the bottle was pointed at me. I swore under my breath, and I spun the bottle. It finally came to a stop and it was pointing at Amanda, the hottest girl in the whole school. I started sweating bullets and waited for her to speak. She asked me "truth or dare?" Me trying to act like a tough guy, I chose dare. Amanda slid her finger up her chest to her lips. She thought for a minute before she rose from the ground. She reached out for my hand. I grabbed it, and she pulled me close and whispered "follow me" in her ear.

Nick -

It wasn't until after my fourth beer pong win that I began to feel sick. As I felt my stomach rumble, I pushed my way past everyone and darted to the front door. As soon as I got outside, I puked my brains out. After I was finally done hurling, I got back up on my feet and took a look around. Everything was blurry. I attempted to make my way back inside, but I tripped over my own two feet, and my head slammed into the concrete; it hurt like a bitch! I raised my hand and felt that my head was bleeding. I brought my hand back to my face to see it painted with my blood. I started to panic, and just as I started to get up, I saw a flashing light behind me. I jumped into the bushes, scraping my body all over. Naturally, I thought it was the cops, but it wasn't. It was a lamp post a few houses down, and its light kept flickering. I was pissed off and felt like an idiot, so I decided to give the shitty lamp post a piece of my mind. I looked on the ground and found a rock. I stumbled towards it and started smashing the rock into the lamp post until its light went out. The moment the light went out, I heard a noise behind me, so I turned around, but I saw nothing. All of a sudden the light began to flicker again. Out of rage, I balled my hand into a fist and turned towards the light. But once I turned, my heart dropped. There was a skinny, bony figure sitting on the top of the lamp post. I opened my mouth to scream, but just before I could, the figure pounced on me and reached its hand down my throat. I began to gag. I couldn't breathe. I felt the creature's hands wiggling inside me. Just as I raised my hands in an attempt to push it off, I felt a puncture in my chest, and I watched as the thing yanked its hand out along with my internal organs. In my last few moments of life, I felt nothing, but just before my vision faded, I saw him bite into my internal organs.

Nate -

It felt like a dream. The hottest girl in the school had whispered in my ear and asked if I wanted to go upstairs with her! I was speechless, but after she studied my face for a moment, she started pulling me along towards the stairs. Once we were upstairs, she shoved me against the bed. She told me "no peeking" while she undressed, so I looked out the window until she was done. I noticed there was a strange flickering light from outside. My eyes followed the source, and it looked to be some type of lamp post. I also noticed something sitting on top of it; it looked deathly skinny. My hands began to shake as I noticed a figure stumbling towards the post. It began hitting the skinny creature, and the light went out. When it turned back on, I saw the figure jump off the post and onto the person. From a distance it looked like it was strangling him, but then I saw it pull out the internal organs! Frozen with terror, I pissed myself as I watched it bite into what looked like its lungs.

I heard Amber announce she was done, and when I turned around I saw her with only a towel wrapped around her. I watched as her smile faded. She looked at my wet shorts, screamed that I was disgusting, grabbed her clothes from the floor, and ran out the room. I was so embarrassed I ran to the bathroom, took off my shorts, and stuffed them in the trash. Just as I began to put on a new pair of shorts, there was a loud bang. I rushed over to the window, and I saw Amanda walking down the street towards the lamp post. When she got within a few feet, she paused and turned back at the house. I swear it felt like she was staring at me. While she stared, I saw the bony creature walk up behind her. Just as she turned around, it grabbed her and snapped her neck. I watched as the figure towered over her body, and its eyes followed the sidewalk back to the house. The creature's gaze went from the sidewalk directly to me, and I dropped to the floor, hoping it didn't see me. I waited a few minutes before I looked out the window again, but when I did, I saw nothing but the flickering lamp post.

I didn't know what to do. I debated calling the cops. Yes, everyone would hate me, but I knew something was very wrong here. So I grew a pair and called 911. I explained how there was a graduation party going on at Saint Randle Street. Stuttering from fear, I managed to inform them that something was wrong. I mentioned how there was something killing people next to a flickering lamp post. The operator asked "Sir, are you drunk?" It took me a minute to process that before I answered no. She sighed and said she would send a car out to the house. I yelled at her that people were dying, so she assured me the police were on their way.

I hung up and slammed my phone on the ground. I rushed down the stairs to see who was left, and I found one of my other friends, Noah. I quickly made my way towards him, and I tapped him on the shoulder, informing him we needed to leave now. When he asked why, I said the cops were on their way. Then he shouted, "You called the cops!?" I punched him in the shoulder, but then everyone started to curse at me and throw trash at me. As people began to flee, one guy decided to shove me into the pool. I entered the water head first and bashed my head at the bottom of the pool..The pain was unbearable. I felt as if I were going to drown, but then suddenly I was picked up and brought out of the water; it was Noah. He immediately apologized for being a dick and claimed he was just in utter shock.

Noah then asked if I was ok as blood trickled down my face. I told him no, so he suggested we get out of here before the police arrive. I muttered no. We needed to stay because I saw a figure on the street killing people. Noah looked at me like I was on crack or something. He asked if I was high, but I yelled no! I told him I knew what I saw, so then he asked what I saw. Just as I opened my mouth to answer, I heard the sirens in the distance.

As Noah helped me up, an officer started sprinting towards me after seeing my injury, and he called for an ambulance while he asked me about what had happened. I told him how I saw an skeletal figure kill two people from the party; he radioed it in, saying he was checking on the possible deaths of two teens. Noah helped me walk over to the sidewalk where I pointed at the flickering lamp post.

We watched as the officer took a look around, and after a few minutes he radioed back, "We have blood; send all available units to my location." Then he turned back towards us. Tears began to trickle down my cheeks as I saw the creature stealthily walk up behind the officer. Noah saw it, too, and screamed, "Behind you!" but by the time the officer turned around, the thing ripped a bone from its rib cage and jabbed it in the officer's face. It crouched over him, ripping him limb from limb and tossing the pieces in a sack that it carried on its back. Then the bony figure grinned and paced towards us. Noah stepped in front of me and told me to run. I stumbled to my feet and began running. I couldn't bear to look back as I heard Noah's screams followed by the sounds of bones snapping. I ran back towards the house. Once I entered, I slammed the door shut and locked it. I began to think of all possible hiding spots in case that thing got inside.

I ran around panicking when I heard movement from outside, and it stopped at the front door. There was a long silence, but I wouldn't dare open the door. I wasn't that stupid. Afraid that the creature was listening for any movement from inside, I stood frozen in place. I noticed the window next to me had its curtains open, so I darted towards them, but when I grabbed both curtains and began to pull them closed, I looked through the window to see the thing staring at me.

I froze in fear, which caused it to smile. I watched as it reached into its sack and pulled out Noah's head! I screamed and sprinted upstairs. I heard the glass shatter behind me, which only made me run faster. I made my way into one of the bedrooms and closed the door, locked it, and began barricading it. I heard on the other side of the wall what sounded like claws scraping the wall as the beast walked nearby. I began to hyperventilate as the door knob started to jiggle. I turned around, opened the window, and climbed out.

I didn't even bother shutting the window behind me. I was running for my life. My only option was to jump from the second story window to the ground. Then a light bulb went off in my head. I climbed up onto the roof and crawled to the back of the house. I did a cannonball from the roof into the pool, so I wouldn't fracture my legs, but my impact resulted in a loud splash. *Great,* I thought, *I just gave away my location.*

I did not waste a second of time. I immediately crawled onto the cement. Once I got myself up, I began to run towards the cop's car. I grabbed the door handle, and the door swung open. I jumped inside, making sure to lock the door behind me. I looked around for the keys, but I didn't find them. However, I did find a radio inside the car, so I clicked the button while shouting, "Code red! Officer down." Someone reported back, asking for my location. I told them Saint Randle Street. I was informed that all available units were being sent to my location. I finally breathed a sigh of relief as I waited for the cops to arrive.

To my surprise, nothing happened while I waited for the police to arrive. I never saw that thing once the cops arrived. They took my statement while dozens of others searched the house and woods behind it. I would say no longer than 15 minutes after they arrived, they came out of the house empty handed.

The supervising officer approached me and asked what sick kind of joke I was pulling here. Then he asked me firmly what happened to Officer Allen. With fear and rage flowing through my veins, I got in the officer's face, while tears rushed down my face, and said I had witnessed that thing kill two of my close friends, my crush, and Officer Allen. Another officer slid between the two of us, telling me to calm down. Then he turned to his fellow officer and told him to lay off since there were still units searching the woods.

Another officer walked me to her car and told me to sit in the back and calm down while they kept searching. I watched the injured officer enter the house; a few moments later he came outside, shaking his head. He approached an officer holding a notepad; that officer began to frantically write down his supervisor's words. After he was done speaking, he made his way to me. He opened the door and apologized for how he acted, but he asked me to understand he had lost one of his fellow officers and had to explain to his boss how four people just disappeared into thin air. Just like that, he walked away. Then the officer who let me sit in her car offered me a ride home. Without hesitation, I responded with a yes, please!

As she pulled away from the curb, I saw the lamp post start flickering again. I screamed, "Look!" She slammed on her brakes and shot her head towards me. She then followed the direction of my hand pointing at the lamp post. She gently reassured me that it was just an old broken lamp post. She told me she would tell her supervisor to get it fixed, but that didn't make me feel any better.

During the entire ride home, my stomach felt queasy. When the officer finally turned down my street, I stuttered, asking if she believed me. I could see her eyes glance up at her mirror while she answered, "Of course I do, honey. Don't you worry; we'll get to the bottom of this."

I thanked the officer. As I formed a fake smile, I pointed out that my house was coming up, so she slowed down and parked in my driveway. She offered to walk me to the door, but I declined it. I watched as her headlights flashed. She pulled out of the driveway and cruised down the street. I quietly made my way up the stairs because I didn't want to wake my parents up. I made my way to my room, where I crawled into bed and proceeded to pass out like a light.

Never Left

I awoke to my mother throwing a pillow at my face, screaming at me to get up. I rolled out of bed only to fall on my floor. My mother shouted that the police were at the door asking for me. I nearly pissed myself again. I had completely forgotten about last night, but then it all came back to me. I nearly levitated off my floor and rushed past my mother, thumping down the stairs all the way to the front door where I saw my father talking to a bunch of cops. The female officer from last night was there. She came up to me and said that I was right about everything. She mentioned how the teams from last night did a second search in the morning and found the remains of four individuals.

I began to cry while she continued on, giving the details about how much was left of each individual. My father gave me a sturdy hug and patted my back. My mother must have heard me crying because she rushed down the stairs to check on me. While both my parents were in the same room,

I began to attempt to tell them about last night, but I couldn't manage to speak, so one of the officers began briefing my parents. I watched my parents' faces twist in disbelief; when the office got to the part where the creature pulled out Nick's organs, my father puked all over the floor.

Before the officer left, one of them informed me that they had sent an electrician to replace the light in the lamp post. For the first time in what felt like forever, I smiled and let out a sigh of relief. I believed the nightmare would finally be over.

Electrician -

It was a slow day when I received a call about needing to replace the bulb of a lamp post. So I agreed to fix it, but I first had to go to the lamp post to figure out which bulb I needed. On the way there it began to get dark, and by the time I finally got there it was pitch black. However, the darkness had no effect on me finding which post was defective because I saw one that kept flickering. I pulled up next to it and got out of my truck. Since it was so dark, I pulled out my flashlight. When I turned it on, I pointed it to the top of the light and saw a thin creature perched at the top, smiling at me.

The Family Tradition

The Family Tradition
Story Summary

Every family has a tradition. For Griffin, his family tradition means moving around alot, making it hard to find friends. Every time he starts to settle in, his father tells him it's time to leave again. Sadly, poor Griffin leaves more than just his friends behind.

Hit The Road

Griffin -

Another year, another new school – that's been the recurring issue for as long I can remember. It's the same thing every year; we move into a new house, and I'm enrolled into the closest school, and by the end of the school year, my father informs me that I need to pack because we need to move again. I never dared to ask why until I was 15 years old. I decided to ask my father's current girlfriend.

I figured she would most likely tell me the truth since my dad has been known to lie about things. When I asked her, she nervously took a glance around the house, probably to see if my father was home. Once she finished looking and found nothing, she began to speak, but before she could even get a few words out, the front door flung open.

It was my dad. He was drenched in sweat and looked severely irritated. His girlfriend welcomed him home with a big hug; then she told my father how I was curious about us moving. My father looked me in the eyes, put his hand on my shoulder and said it was because of his job, that it requires him to move around a lot. At the time, I thought it made sense, so I smiled. My father then asked me to go upstairs and finish packing.

I trampled up the stairs and went into my room. I jumped on my bed and took a look around to see what still needed to be packed. The only things that were not yet packed were a few of my video games. I hopped off my bed and began putting them into a box when I heard screaming followed by a loud thud. I was not scared.

I knew what that meant, so I gathered all my things and sat on my bed until father opened my door, saying, "Time to hit the road, kiddo." He walked into my room and picked up all my things. I followed him down the stairs and glanced at his girlfriend. She lay there, her neck spewing blood. I made sure to not step in the pool of blood on my way out the door while my father dragged her body to the basement. My father waited until we got in the car, his eyes pierced against the rearview mirror. He told me that she was just like the rest of them. I frowned. I had liked her the best out of all of his previous girlfriends. My father told me to cheer up. He would soon find a perfect replacement for my real mother. He muttered, "I have to. It's my job."

ZaKiki Island

ZaKiki Island
Story Summary

Escaping everyday life by going on vacation is an amazing opportunity not everyone gets. David and his family go to a tropical island as his graduation gift. It's an absolutely beautiful place, but it's not until David and his family go on a safari that they realize it's not life they should be escaping, but their vacation.

Summer Time

David -

The sun's rays were burning my skin to a crisp, so I decided to go back inside to avoid getting sunburnt. I stood up and let out a yawn as I stretched. I walked towards the house and slid my glass patio door open just enough for me to squeeze through.

I swear not even a second after I entered, I was greeted by Rex, my 85 pound golden retreiver. Rex stood on his hind legs while his paws punched my stomach, his tail wagging enthusiastically as he panted. I placed my hand on his head and scratched behind his ear. Rex has been my dog ever since elementary school, and we have a strong relationship, but I yelled "Down!" Rex immediately lay on the floor. He knew the drill; if he listened that meant he would get a treat. So I asked him to do a few more things, like "Speak" and "Paw," while I got his cookie. Rex devoured the cookie like it was the last one on earth. I chuckled and went into my room.

I pushed the door open and turned on the air conditioning because my skin still felt like it was on fire. Well, that's what I get for lying in the sun during the summer. Speaking of summer, I actually just graduated high school last year, so this is the last summer before I start college. I've always been a straight A student, so my parents decided that we would take a family vacation to wherever I wanted as a reward. Since I had nothing else to do, I decided to look at potential destinations.

I was looking at pictures of places on Google but saw nothing breathtaking, but then just before I closed my laptop, an ad popped up for an island. It was a beautiful place. The ad read, "Trying to get away for the summer but can't find the perfect spot? Well, we've got just the place for you: ZaKiki Island." I couldn't help but look up more pictures of the island. It was absolutely beautiful. I decided in just minutes that was the place that I wanted to go.

I called my mom, telling her I found the best place. I told her the name of the island and how beautiful it was. She told me that she had never heard of a "ZaKiki Island," so she asked me to look at the reviews first. I objected, telling her that I was told I got to pick where we would go since it was my gift. There was silence before my mother spoke again. She told me that if that's really where I wanted to go, we could. I shouted, "Let's go!" I thanked her and told her I loved her before hanging up. I didn't waste a second; after I hung up, I informed my father that I had chosen ZaKiki Island, and he responded with, "Interesting. I've never heard of it, but it sounds like a nice place." Just as I was dancing around the house, I heard keys jingling.

The door then squeaked open, and my sister walked in with a weird expression. She asked, "Why are you dancing? You're a weirdo." That's when I told her where we were going, but she didn't seem to care until I showed her a picture of the place. Her attitude changed, and she smiled and said, "Oh my God. It's beautiful!"

My sister asked, "How did you find this place?" I told her how the ad just popped up on my screen so I couldn't help but look at it. My sister asked how the reviews were. I shrugged, saying I didn't look yet. My sister exited my room then reappeared in my doorway. She had her glasses on with her laptop in her hands. We just stared at each other for a moment before I broke the silence. I asked her what she was doing. She sat on my bed and invited me to sit next to her. Again, I asked her, "What are you doing?"

Finally she answered, claiming that she was getting a weird feeling about how such a beautiful Island just popped up on my screen, and how no one's ever heard of it, so she told me that she was going to look up some reviews. I told her that she was just wasting time. I already determined that was where we would be going, but I don't think she really cared about what I said because she continued searching for reviews. She wasn't finding much of anything, so I shrugged and decided to take a trip to the bathroom.

I was only in there for a few minutes, so I was surprised when I heard my sister mumbling. I was starting to get sick of this, so I barged into my own room, but before I could yell at her, I couldn't help but notice the fear in her eyes. She must have heard my footsteps because her head snapped towards me, and she began to cry. I rushed to her side and asked what the matter was. With hands trembling, she pointed to the screen.

I glanced at an article and attempted to read it but stopped cold at the title. "Remains of missing person found on ZaKiki Island." After rereading the title 50 times, I was finally able to regain my focus. I began reading the article, and it just kept getting worse and worse. My sister and I glanced at each other. She mumbled that this article was from 2019, only four years ago. I couldn't believe my eyes. How could such a beautiful place be so scary? After reading the article, I was hesitant to choose the island, but I remembered something my grandfather used to tell me: "David, there are always two sides to a story."

So keeping that in mind, I decided to look more into the incident, and the island itself, before I made any decisions. After about 30 mintues of research, I found another article claiming that the remains were not human. It said the remains were from a chimpanzee, an animal that roams freely around the island.

Plus, it said those bones had been there long before the individual went missing. After I read this, I felt stupid for immediately believing the gruesome article was automatically true; however, I knew my sister would be hesitant to believe this, so I spent more time looking for reviews. Eventually, I found some under a post about the island. There were about ten to twelve reviews, and I read each one. All of the reviews were positive; people claimed they got to go on a safari and interact with wild animals while also learning the history of the island. Some of the reviews even had pictures attached with ordinary people playing with monkeys.

I smiled and closed the laptop. I shouted loud enough so anyone who was home could hear me, "I've made my decision, We're going to ZaKiki Island." My sister looked at me, asking if I was sick or if I found it amusing to say such a thing. I told her that I did more research, and it turns out it was just an animal. She shook her head while calling me stupid, but before she left, I said, "Look!"
She turned around and took the laptop from my hands.

I could tell she was relieved as she let out a deep breath. I waited while she read the reviews, and a few seconds later, she looked up at me and said, "Okay. Let's go."

Just as my sister finished her sentence, headlights shot through the window, blinding us. It was our parents. We quickly agreed to show our parents the reviews, but only the reviews. My mother walked in the door first while talking to dad about the vacation, so we told them we found some reviews. At first mom was skeptical, but after my father read them, he convinced her to relax a little bit and to stop stressing herself out so much.

Carissa -

"Come on, Mom. Dad's right. Plus this is the last family vacation before David goes to college." I even put on my pouty face. Our mother sighed and whispered ok. I looked at David and gave him a wink; he smiled back at me, mouthing a thank you.

"So then, when are we going to leave?" My mom started to reply, saying she didn't know, but then our dad talked over her, stating that we could leave tomorrow night. I watched as our parents stared at each other, but then mom finally said, "Yeah, ok."

I waited until our parents left the room before I approached my brother. I told him he owed me one and turned toward the stairs. David asked what I was doing. "Ugh! I'm going to bed; it's 10:58 PM."

David -

Carissa's voice became muffled as she went upstairs. I heard her door close, and I looked around. I was alone. I glanced at the clock and figured I should probably go to bed as well since we all had a lot of packing to do tomorrow. Rex followed me up the stairs and into my room. I crawled into bed, and Rex climbed up next to me. I looked at Rex, and he looked at me. He whined, then lay his head down. I scratched behind his ears until I fell asleep.

Free Flight

David -

I woke up at 7 AM thanks to Rex whimpering and needing to go to the bathroom. I groaned and rolled out of bed. I grabbed his leash, attaching it to his collar. I opened the door, and the smell of freshly cooked bacon swirled up my nostrils. I smiled, but then I questioned why I was smelling bacon at seven in the morning. I ran down the steps and poked my head into the kitchen. My jaw dropped because my sister was cooking breakfast! I thought I was dreaming because she sleeps in till noon every day and hates cooking. Carissa saw me and greeted me with a good morning. She must have seen I was confused because she said, "No, you're not dreaming. I just wanted to do something nice for once."

I didn't know how to respond, but then Rex whined again and began pulling me to the door. After Rex went about his business, I went inside, ate breakfast, and began packing. I put the last few things in my suitcase, zipped it up, and looked outside. It was already getting dark. I paused and wondered how long I'd been packing. Suddenly, I was interrupted by my father's booming voice. He shouted "Come on! Let's go!" I grabbed all my things and went down the stairs. Carissa was right behind me. Once everyone was out, our mom locked the door, and we all got in the truck.

The car ride was only five minutes; yet it felt like hours. We had a hard time finding parking, so we had to park across the street; we entered the airport, got through security, and went to the terminal. We waited a long time but never heard our flight being called. We all grew impatient because the wait became unbearable. Finally, the attendant approached us and said there was an unexpected issue with the original plane, so they offered to fly us first class in a small plane.

My mother looked very confused, but they reassured us that they felt terrible for making us wait so long and said it was the least they could do. No one moved until my father said, "You heard the man; let's go!" We followed the attendant down a small hallway where we were guided into a plane. Another attendant insisted on taking our bags. My mother refused, but my father said, "That would be great! Thanks." I watched the man struggle to transfer all our luggage to the back, and I nearly jumped out of my seat when the pilot spoke over the intercom.

"Welcome, everyone! This is your pilot speaking. We apologize for the delays. Please buckle up and relax." A loud clicking sound echoed through the plane, and then the engine sputtered to life and the plane slowly lurched into the air. My dad must have seen the fear in our mother's eyes because he cracked a dad joke, trying to get a laugh out of her, but she didn't. She just sat there.

Then the plane began to violently shake, and one of the attendants fell over. It wasn't until my mother began to scream that my father finally realized something was not right. He unbuckled himself and climbed over towards the flight attendant. Just before he confronted the attendant, the plane rumbled again, knocking my dad flat on his ass. Once the plane was balanced, he got up and began confronting the attendant. He bellowed, "What the hell was that?" but the attendent just stood there, and I swear I saw a single tear drop trickle down his face. I looked around, but nobody seemed to be paying attention. When I looked back, I saw the flight attendant knock on the door to the cockpit before entering.

I sat there, questioning whether I really saw the tear. I convinced myself I must have imagined it since it just didn't make any sense. Then I was startled by someone touching my shoulder. I craned my neck to my right and was relieved to see it was just my father. He explained that we were flying through a storm, and that's what caused the shaking. My sister asked how he knew, and he claimed that it was what the attendant told him after he excited the cockpit. Static interrupted the conversation, and our pilot began to speak. He reiterated that we were flying through a storm and that it seemed we would be out of it soon. In the meantime, snacks and refreshments would be served momentarily.

Just after the intercom clicked off, another flight attendant appeared with a cart containing refreshments and what looked like menus. The woman stopped the cart next to us, asking if we would like anything. She told us we could order anything free of charge, complimentary from the pilot for the delays and the shaking of the plane. No one had a chance to answer before she handed us menus. My mother gasped, "They have steak!" The woman smiled and added that any alcoholic beverage was complimentary as well. My mother elbowed my father, saying that maybe this vacation wasn't so bad after all. The woman wrote down our orders and disappeared.

Only a few minutes after taking our order, she reappeared; the cart was loaded with steaks, sodas, and liquor. My father spoke first. "Well, that was fast!" The woman smiled and informed us we would be landing within the hour. The steaks looked strange but smelled delicious, although they did have a unique texture. Just as my mother finished her drink, the intercom crackled.

"The plane will begin landing momentarily. Please make sure you're buckled up." The plane began to vibrate, but not too badly. My father said it was just normal turbulence. Finally, I felt the tires bounce off the ground, the plane stopped, and the intercom clicked: "Welcome to ZaKiki Island; we hope you enjoy the rest of your vacation."

The flight attendant that served us confirmed it was ok to unbuckle our seat belts. As we made our way to the terminal, the female attendant grasped my mother's hand and suggested we stay at the ZaKiki hotel. She even gave her a brochure.

We followed my father out of the terminal and began looking for the baggage claim. While we looked, we were approached by a nicely dressed man with glasses; he claimed how nice it was to see us and how excited he was that we chose ZaKiki Island. My father looked confused just like the rest of us, and he asked the man where we would find our luggage. He assured us not to worry – that all of our things would be transferred to the ZaKiki hotel.

My mother interrupted him, saying we didn't know exactly where we would stay yet, but the man reiterated how nice the hotel was, and he said it was complimentary.

Carissa -

I was getting suspicious of all this complimentary crap, so I asked the man why everything seemed to be complimentary. My mother whispered in my ear, "Don't argue; it's free." The man started chuckling and said he believed in a vacation being as enjoyable as possible, and that they were trying to attract more tourists.

David -

I was relieved to know my sister had the same question I did, but I didn't really like the man's reaction. After the man finished chuckling, my father asked where we could rent a car. Again the man smiled and said, "We have dune buggies, and they are also complimentary. Please follow me. I'll let you pick one out."

We followed the stranger outside of the airport where we saw dozens of dune buggies. The man grinned and said, "Pick your poison."

My mother immediately saw one she liked, which meant that was the one we would get. The stranger claimed it was a great choice and pulled out a set of keys from his pocket, tossing them to my father. Before disappearing, he gave us directions to our hotel. My parents thanked him, and we all got in the vehicle.

My mother's attitude had completely changed. She was actually having a good time, and she told me that I had been right about this place after all.

In just a few minutes, we arrived at ZaKiki hotel. Once we got there, my father parked the dune buggy and we all went inside. My mouth nearly dropped to the floor. The inside was incredibly beautiful; the decor had a shiny metallic tint to it, and there was a huge, all-day buffet.

There were a few other residents roaming around, but the way they looked at us bothered me; it felt as if they were looking through my skin. I felt uncomfortable and walked closer to my dad as he approached the front desk.

Before he could even ring the bell, he was greeted with a hello. My dad didn't even get to speak before the doorman said "Room 63" and handed him a key. My father asked when our stuff would be transferred. The person smiled and claimed it would be within the hour. My mother thanked him and led the way to the elevator.

I watched as the dial went from the top floor to the lobby. It made a loud ding before opening, classic. We shuffled into the elevator, and my sister pressed the sixth floor button. The doors closed, and we began to ascend.

Suddenly, the elevator came to a stop, the doors opened, and a wealthy looking family entered. My mother tried greeting them, but they just stared at her. Finally, the elevator stopped, and we got out, excited. My sister was the last one out.

Carissa -

When the elevator stopped, this rich family entered, and I got chills down to my spine. They ignored my mother when she tried starting a conversation. Once the elevator stopped at our floor, I followed my brother out, and before the doors closed, I looked back and saw the young boy licking his lips while his mother grinned. I nearly shit myself.

David -

My father stopped to read the numbers on the doors. He scratched his head and turned right down a long hallway. We followed him down the hall until my mother spotted our room.

Our mother inserted the key and pushed on the door, but it didn't budge so she rammed her shoulder into it; she went flying inside and landed on the floor. My father immediately helped her up, making sure she was ok. We all looked around the room and then at each other. It was beautiful.

We all kicked off our shoes and claimed our rooms. I pounced on my bed, laying my face against the plushy pillow. Finally, I was able to relax.

It's Complimentary

David -

I was awoken by my sister. I noticed that she had a very concerned look on her face. When I grunted, "What do you want?" She whispered how strange it was that we still hadn't gotten our luggage. I shrugged and told her to take a chill pill and relax. She looked at me, and I felt her eyes pierce through my skin. She told me something was wrong. She then told me about the rich family in the elevator and how they made creepy facial expressions.

While my sister was freaking out, a phone rang. It rang twice before someone picked it up. There was silence, but then a minute later our mother shouted, "David!"

I groaned and pushed my sister out of my way. She frowned at me and flipped me off as I left the room. My mother was standing in the kitchen, and once she saw me, she claimed that the front desk called. Our things were waiting for us next to the lobby.

She asked if I could go down to make sure everything was there.

I sighed and rolled my eyes. She handed me a room key and thanked me. I shuffled to the door and opened it. I let the door close behind me. Exhausted, I had to use the signs on the walls to find my way to the elevator. I pressed the button and waited; it made the same noise as last time, and the doors slid open. I pressed the button for the lobby and waited for the doors to close.

Finally the doors closed, and the elevator descended. When the doors opened, I was startled by a sickly looking woman who appeared to be in her mid 40s. She looked me up and down and told me to leave while I still could, and then she began to cry. Before I could respond, what looked like one of the building's workers grabbed her by her shirt. He told her that she knew she wasn't allowed to be here, and she needed to leave immediately. She squirmed out of his grip and ran like a bat out of hell out the door.

I stood there frozen. I watched as the man stared after her, making sure she was gone. The man then looked at me and began apologizing, saying that she was just a crazy woman who would come in the hotel and try to scare people away. I nodded and asked where I could pick up my luggage. He smiled and said "Follow me." He brought me right to the room where they kept everyone's things. He offered to grab the luggage for me, but I declined. His smile faded, as he said "Oh, ok. Well, let me know if you need anything."

I thanked him, then entered the room. I strolled down the hall and saw dozens of lockers overstuffed with belongings. I was really surprised by that because I had only seen one other family here.

It took me a while, but I finally spotted them because my sister's obnoxious violet-colored case was on top. I knew there was no way in hell I could transport all of our things in one trip. I sighed and swore as I realized I would be making several trips. The only damn thing I wanted was to relax, but of course, I had to do everything.

I decided I wasn't going to make more than one trip, so I dragged bag after bag to the elevator where I pulled them all in with me. I pressed the button for our floor, and the doors closed. The elevator made its ding sound, and the doors slid open.

It was a struggle, but I finally was able to grab everything at once. I looked up, and standing in front of me was a very pale man; he looked deathly ill. He raised one finger, shushing me. When I walked past him, he grabbed my shoulder. I thrust myself forward, breaking from his grasp. He whispered to wait, but I kept on going. I got to the room and knocked on the door. While I waited for the door to open, I glanced down the hall behind me, and I saw the old man still standing there, shaking.

Finally, the door handle turned as I barged my way in and dropped everything on the floor. I then locked the door. I turned around to see my sister. She asked, "What happened out there?" I couldn't speak. It was late, so I just walked past her and went straight to bed.

I woke up to my sister shaking me. I slapped her arms away, but she didn't stop. I rolled out of bed and asked what the hell she wanted. She told me that mom had won some raffle, and she had four one-day passes to attend the island's safari. I wondered when our mom ever entered a raffle. My sister asked if I planned on going. I told her that this place was weird, and the last thing I wanted to do was go on some safari.

Carissa -

I whispered in my brother's ear, telling him that we both knew this place was weird, but did he really want to spend the day in the room alone? His face went pale.

David -

I thought there was no way in hell I was going on some safari, but after my sister asked if I really wanted to be alone in the room all day, I thought of the creepy people I saw last night, and I felt myself turn pale. I changed my mind. "I'll go."

She claimed we were leaving soon, so I excused myself and went along with my morning routine. I got ready and decided to lie on my bed and relax a little. Of course, just as I lay down, my father shouted, "Let's go! We don't want to miss our tour!" I rolled my eyes and sprung off the bed. My father called my name, telling me to hurry up.

I left my room, carrying a sling bag over my shoulder with everything I felt I needed: a hat, sunglasses, sunscreen, and camera. I met my sister in the kitchen. She was standing there alone. She urged me to hurry up because mom and dad were already downstairs waiting for us.

She pushed the door open and said, "Ladies first." I glared at her as I went into the hall. Once I was in the hallway, she closed the door and locked it.

Carissa -

"Ok, let's go."

David -

We strode down the hall to the elevator. I pushed the button. We heard the ding, and the doors opened.

We entered, but just as the door began to close, a hand shot through, stopping it. The doors opened again, and a freakishly tall man entered. He looked sick; he was so thin you could see the bones under his skin. "Hello," he whispered.

I looked at him, and his mouth cracked into a smile. He began to pat me on the head, while saying "Oh Alex, is that you?" I smacked his hand away and told him to keep his hands off me. When the elevator stopped, the man looked confused and cried, "I'm sorry, Alex. I won't leave you ever again." I shoved him and told him to get away from me. Moments later, the elevator doors opened. The old man limped out, muttering how he wished he would've gone on that damn safari.

As soon as the creepy old twig exited, we made a beeline for the lobby where we met our parents.

My sister and I both began to panic while trying to tell our parents about the creepy man; however, our father interrupted, scolding us and telling us how we were going to be late, and that he didn't want to hear any excuses. I tried to object, but my father grabbed me by the shoulder and told me to shut up.

It took everything in me not to cry; my sister reached for my hand, and we followed our parents out the door.

Once we walked outside, we were met by a small group of men standing near a dune buggy. One of them smiled and approached my father, shaking his hand. He introduced himself as our tour guide. He directed us to our seats and began asking us a few "precautionary questions."

Our parents didn't seem to be bothered by the questions they were asking. It wasn't until they asked for our phones that I erupted. I tried climbing out of the vehicle, but my father put me in a choke hold and whispered to knock it off. When he let me go, everyone was staring at me, even my sister. I handed my phone to my father, who gave it to our guide.

The guide did his best to change the mood. He explained how each week they held a raffle that consisted of some prize, and that this week it was the safari. He reminded us that only one family could win the raffle a week, so we should consider ourselves lucky. I noticed my mother's smile retreating from her face. I could tell she felt insulted by his comment.

Our guide glanced around before putting the keys in the ignition; the doom buggy sputtered to life and began to rumble. Our guide turned back towards us, smiled, and stepped on the gas.

As our guide was driving, he began giving us the history of the island and suggested we look at the breathtaking views around us. We all looked around, but there were only trees and grass.

Carissa -

I cleared my throat, "Oh yeah, I've never seen trees before." My mother glared at me and mouthed at me to stop. I looked back at my brother who was just staring off into the wilderness.

Suddenly, our vehicle came to an abrupt stop. Our guide turned around and smiled. "Well, here we are."

David -

I began to laugh when my father asked if this was some kind of joke. The man's smile faded, "No, it's not a joke, so you'd better start running. A grin formed on the guide's face as he whipped out a dagger and swung it at my mother.

My father grasped the man by his neck and slammed him into a tree. The man just chuckled and looked me right in my eyes. He claimed I should have just stayed in the room like the other residents did.

My father punched the man square in his face. Blood trickled down his face, but he still smiled. "You know, those old people you met? They decided to stay in their rooms as their loved ones went on the safari. Poor Albert. I'm sure he is still looking for his grandson Alex." While the man was smiling at us, we quickly jumped out of the vehicle and made a run for it.

David -

I started hyperventilating once I realized what was happening. I turned back towards the vehicle and told my dad that we needed to get out of here. I looked at my sister and mother as they stumbled towards the buggy.

Carissa -

I began to feel dizzy from thinking about what could've possibly happened to the old man's poor grandson. I sprinted towards the vehicle, climbing in while my mother did the same. We needed to get the fuck out of here!

I watched as our father threw the man to the ground and began to sprint towards us, but before he could get to us, there was a loud bang, and his head exploded!

I couldn't believe my eyes. I began hysterically crying, but what was even worse was when I looked up, I saw the little rich boy from the elevator holding a pistol.

I screeched and told my brother to drive, but there was no response. I turned around and saw the rich father strangling David and the rich mother carving up my mother's chest.

I shrieked and jumped out of the vehicle. I watched as my brother squirmed in the rich man's grasp, but I knew I was helpless. So I took off into the woods where I could hear little kid footsteps crunching branches behind me. He told me to stop running. I swore at him, telling him to go to hell, and I began running faster.

I ran so fast that my chest felt like it was about to explode. I finally had to stop to catch my breath. I knew I wasn't going to be able to run anymore, so I glanced around, looking for a place to hide. I noticed a fallen tree surrounded by some tall grass, but before I made it there, something grabbed me from behind and covered my mouth. A woman's voice shushed me and told me to be quiet. She instructed me to lie down in the grass and not to move. I didn't know what to do, so I complied. We lay there for what felt like several minutes when I heard footsteps again.

I heard a little boy's voice asking for me to come out. The woman tightened her hand around my mouth while whispering to be quiet.

There was a long silence, before I heard the footsteps again. I listened to them as they faded into the distance. Once it was dead silent, the woman removed her hands from me. I turned my head slightly to see a middle aged mother who looked very ill.

She told me not to scream. She was only trying to help. She told me how she met my brother when he came to get all of our luggage and begged him to leave. She also told me how one of the workers tackled her and dragged her away from him.

I began sobbing. I asked her what this place was, and what was happening? She sniffled and claimed that this was a private island that belonged to a rich family who were cannibals.

I couldn't speak. I felt so bad. Just when I thought the worst was over, she apologized. I looked at her and asked why she was sorry. She told me this was the only way she could get her family back.

I didn't understand what she meant, but before I could figure it out, someone wrapped a chain around my neck and pulled it tight. I gasped for air, but it only made things worse. Right before I passed out, I saw the rich mother thank the ill woman, claiming she was the best actor yet! Everything was becoming muffled. I couldn't see much of anything, and then everything went black.

Dinner

Carissa -

I was awoken by a loud bang; standing in front of me was the little rich boy with a gun. He told me how he thought I was cute, and if I behaved he wouldn't kill me. I then realized I was shackled to a table. I screamed as loud as I could, but the little kid mumbled that he warned me.

He fired the gun again, and immediately several waiters came in and pushed me out of the room. They brought me to a kitchen, where I saw the entire rich family standing. The mother told me that my family was quite delicious, and she was hopeful I would taste even better. I screamed as they picked out which parts of me they wanted to eat, and then I saw one of the waiters raise a saw.

Pysch Ward

Psych Ward Story Summary

The year was 1901 when the Milroy Psych Ward was opened. Milroy reached its full capacity of patients only five years after opening. In 1909, a male nurse leaked what was really going on inside the ward. However, before authorities had the chance to enter, there was a terrible fire, killing everyone inside. Authorities never entered the ward because they deemed it unsafe, but in 2004, almost 100 years later, a couple decided it would be fun to enter the abandoned ward. Once inside, they realized it was not the rotting infrastructure they needed to worry about.

2004

Ryan -

I was high as a kite when I thought it would be a good idea to go exploring in some abandoned building. I shouted for my girlfriend Fiona while I was hacking from the smoke filling my lungs.

Fiona looked so beautiful like she always did. She stumbled into my room, asking what I wanted. I told her I had an idea as I took another hit from my joint. She stood there looking at me. "Well, what is it?" I opened my mouth to answer and started coughing again. I told her we should go exploring.

Fiona looked at me, intrigued. I told her we should go to the Milroy Asylum. Her eyes dilated, and she told me that the place burned almost 100 years ago, and that there was probably nothing there to discover. I couldn't help but laugh.

She sat down in the bed and began playing with my long hair. I went to take another hit, but she stopped me. She looked me in the eyes while she took a hit from the joint. She blew the gray clouds in my face before we kissed.

We continued smoking the joint until there was nothing left of it. We kissed again and she batted her eyes at me, "Well, what are we waiting for? Let's go." She giggled as she got up and fixed her shirt. I rolled off the bed and walked up behind her as she was looking in the mirror. I kissed the top of her head, reached for her hand, and pulled her into the hallway.

I coughed as I made my way to the kitchen. I grabbed my keys from the top of my fridge, and pushed the door open while Fiona waited for me to lock the door. I shoved my keys into my jeans and took her hand as we descended down the stairs.

Once we were outside, I felt a sharp cold wind scratch my face. I looked to see Fiona shivering, so I grasped her hand as we walked to my car.

My car was old, but it still did its job. It took a minute for the heater to kick on, but it eventually did. I looked at Fiona, and shouted, "Milroy, here we come!" Fiona cheered as I shifted the car into drive. I stepped on the gas, and the car bounced as we flew down the dirt roads.

1900

Zach -

It was Christmas of 1900 when I was hired to be one of the nurses inside the Milroy asylum. I was hired by a man named Milroy. He never exactly explained what his profession was, but considering he always wore aprons, I figured he was a doctor.

Milroy explained his visions of the asylum to me while he gave me a tour throughout the facility. At the time, it was empty. No patients had been admitted yet because Mr Milroy was still hiring staff. The tour was over two hours long, not because the building was so vast, but because he would show me the equipment in each room and what it would be used for.

Some of the things he was saying made me sick to my stomach, and at one point I interrupted. I argued that the machines he was showing me were unethical to use on a living being. Milroy stared at me, reminding me how the people who would be admitted were defective and that it would be our job to fix them. Milroy patted me on the back and continued with the tour.

Once the tour was over, Milroy handed me a uniform and informed me all nurses were required to live in the asylum. Before I could object, he assured me not to worry. He motioned for me to follow him so he could show me where I would be sleeping.

2004

Ryan -

The asylum was only about fifteen minutes away, so we got there without a problem. The only challenge we faced was when I pulled into the long driveway because the building was barricaded by barbed wire.

We stared at the fence, wondering how we could get in. Fiona suggested we should just go home. I immediately told her no. I've been breaking into abandoned places for years, and there's always a way in; we just had to find it.

1902

Zach -

In 1901, we nearly shut down because we had only four patients emitted, and Milroy was struggling to fund his dream.

However, in 1902, a rich family who had a rebellious son came to Milroy. The family begged us to fix their son; they thought he might have been possessed. They paid $50,000 hoping we could fix him. Milroy assured them that we would fix their son.

Months later, the boy showed absolutely no signs of getting any better. I used all the tactics I learned in school, but nothing worked. When I told Milroy I couldn't fix the boy, he asked if I was using the machinery he had bought. I told him no, and it was like a fuse went off inside him. He grabbed me by the shirt and pushed me against the wall. He reminded me how much money he spent on this place and how we needed to fix that boy or we would go bankrupt. He released me from his grip and demanded I follow him.

I watched as he entered the boy's room and grabbed him by his color. The boy tried to escape

Milroy's grasp, but he couldn't. I watched Milroy as he dragged the patient down the hall into one of the operating rooms. He slammed the boy on a table and restrained his arms and legs. Milroy demanded that I restrain the boy's head. So I pressed down on the boy's head, keeping him still. I watched as Milroy grabbed some type of sharp rusty pipe and jammed it in the boy's eye.

Blood spewed on all of us, but the boy's screams were much more terrifying. Milroy said if I wanted the child to live, I shouldn't let him move, so I used all my strength to keep the boy's head from moving. His ear-piercing screams made my ears bleed, but after a few minutes, the boy stopped screaming, so Milroy removed the pipe. He wrapped layers and layers of gauze around the boy's eye. He instructed me to bring the boy back to his room and to clean myself up.

I asked if the boy was dead. Milroy assured me he wasn't; all he did was perform a lobotomy. He smiled and told me the boy would no longer be rebellious. A few weeks later, the boy's parents came to check on him. They were concerned about the scars on his face, but Milroy informed them that the operation they did would prevent him from being bad again. Their family smiled and hugged Milroy. They assured him that they would make sure everyone would hear about this beautiful place. Milroy smiled while they signed the release papers and thanked them for coming here.

2004

Fiona -

I started to regret agreeing to come here. I admit I get scared easily, but I've never felt as scared as I was right now. As the wind blew, I could swear I heard voices, and when I looked up at the building, I saw something move behind a window. I tugged on Ryan's hoodie and told him I was getting a bad feeling about this place. He told me not to worry. He would protect me from whatever rodents were inside. I said ok, and I sat down on the ground as I watched him use a knife to cut the fence.

Finally, the old fence gave, and there was a small hole. Ryan lay on his back and kicked the small opening over and over. After about five kicks, the fence ripped apart, making an opening big enough for us to get in.

The excitement on Ryan's face as he was able to get us in made me smile. I decided I wasn't going to let my feelings ruin his mood. We crawled through the fence and approached the building.

1903

Zach -

To my surprise, the family actually spread the news about this place and rich families from across the country began bringing their loved ones here.

The ward was at 75% of its capacity, and there was not enough staff to efficiently treat all these patients. The lack of staff led to a lot of abuse and neglect. There were only about 20 nurses working on 150 patients.

Everyone brought here was suffering from different issues, so they required different operations and treatments. After seeing Milroy perform on that boy and it being a success, I started to trust he knew what he was talking about. So as he wanted me to do, I began using the machinery and inhumane tactics to fix these people.

There was one man who refused to speak; according to his records he was antisocial and committed cruel actions. At the time, it was not uncommon for people to be antisocial, or for their families to send them away to asylums like ours.

However, I wasn't quite sure how to treat this man, so I asked Milroy, and he told me to watch. Milroy grabbed a blade and began slashing the man's arms, and legs, forcing him to scream, as his arms and legs gushed blood.

Milroy looked at me and claimed the issue with this man was that he was possessed by some evil spirit. Therefore, he insisted that the man needed to be brutally tortured so whatever spirit possessed him would hopefully leave. Milroy instructed me to make him suffer as much as possible, and at some point, the evil spirit would have to leave. Milroy handed me the blade and watched me as I slashed the man's body. There were pools of blood under the chair he was restrained in.

Finally, the man passed out, and Milroy told me to get him cleaned up. I did as he said and brought the man back to his room. Just before I left his room, he regained consciousness and began to beg that I let him go. I stared at him and asked if he still felt like hurting people? He looked at me, and shook his head yes, so I grabbed a whip, and began whipping him until he changed his mind.

After about 10 slashes, the man changed his mind and finally spoke, promising he felt like a changed man, so I cleaned him up and made sure he was comfortable. Then I called Dr. Milroy and asked him to check on him. Milroy was pleased with what he saw; he did some tests to see if the man was lying, but he seemed to be telling the truth, so I gathered his release forms.

Right before that man was released, I told him to not tell anyone about what had happened here, and he would never have to come back here again. The man nodded and was brought to his family.

The more patients we admitted, the worse my methods of treatment became. Milroy began praising me, calling me one of his favorite nurses; however, there was one other nurse he favored more, Ben. Ben was the worst of us all. He went above and beyond what Milroy expected; he found pleasure in torturing his patients. I never found pleasure in anything I did. I only did what I did because I really believed I was helping people. After all, 75% of our patients who came in were released.

Milroy knew I feared Ben, so he had us partner up on the worst patients we had. They were kept in a different part of the ward because Milroy feared if they were exposed to the others, they might make things worse. Milroy guided us to the basement where we kept the ones who didn't leave this place.

I saw the patients lying on the floors of their rooms, some of them rocking with their faces tucked in their arms. Others just cackled, and a few were mute.

We stopped at a patient named Jane. Milroy told us how Jane suffered from severe depression and refused to talk. He asked if we could fix her. We nodded, so he threw us the keys and said we had better.

Ben looked at me and told me to go set up the operating room. I complied. When I had finished setting up the tool kit that we used, Ben came in with the woman on his shoulder. He threw her in the chair and looked at the tools I laid out. He swore that these tools were not going to fix anything.

I watched him as he began searching the room, and the woman looked at me and whispered for help. Ben must have heard because he turned around and punched her square in the face. He told her to shut up. I grabbed Ben by the arm and insisted it was a good thing that she spoke; however, Ben didn't agree. He pushed her to the ground and shoved a cloth in her mouth. Then he threw me the keys and told me to get started on the next patient.

As I left the room, I decided to take one last look before leaving, and I saw Ben raping her while he tortured her. I was going to throw up, so I ran upstairs and puked into a laundry bin.

I saw Milroy talking to another nurse. Once he saw me, he approached me and asked how everything was coming along. I told him what Ben was doing, but he seemed unfazed; he simply reiterated that we needed to fix these people, and we needed to do whatever it took. He told me to get back down there because we had another patient on the way.

He walked me back down into the basement and told me to take care of the ones who were left. He reminded me that if I could help them, then Ben wouldn't have to. Milroy left me down there alone. I walked back along the rooms, and I saw the mute girl lying on her bed with the cover over her. I unlocked the door and pulled the sheets down to see that her face was gray. She was dead.

I pulled the sheet back over her face, locked her door, and made my way to the operating room. The closer I got, the worse the sounds were, but what I saw was far worse than the screams I heard. I peeked through the glass of the operating room door, and I saw three people in there. One Ben was electrocuting. He had another on a table that stretches the limbs and pulls them out of their sockets. The last one I saw was a woman, chained to the ground. I watched as Ben began whipping her. Then he climbed on top of her and committed foul acts I refuse to describe.

I thought about what Milroy said, so I walked back down the hall to see if there were any patients left. I found one; she was rocking violently, I looked at her chart. Her name was Veronica, she was 25, and her chart said she had been admitted by her husband for attempting to stab him.

I unlocked the door and told her to get off the ground. She sprang off the ground and charged at me, knocking me over. I was able to restrain her by putting her in a chokehold, and I brought her to the other operating room. I pushed her against the wall and handcuffed her. I then shoved her into a chair. I decided I would try a lobotomy since it fixed our first patient.

I couldn't find anything to use, so I took a long pair of scissors and jammed them in her eye. She screamed bloody murder, and she kept moving her head back and forth. I told her to stop, but she kept screaming. Her screams hurt my ears, so I jammed the scissors farther into her skull, and they penetrated her brain. She immediately went quiet while blood oozed down her face.

I didn't know what to do, so I yanked the scissors from her skull, and blood just gushed everywhere. I wrapped her face in layers of gauze and a few towels, and then I carried her back to her room. Ben was waiting for me, asking why I took her. I replied that I wasn't going to let him have all the fun. I asked him what to do with the bodies. He told me to drag them to the furnace, and he would burn them. So I dragged all the bodies to the furnace and helped him toss body after body inside. After all the bodies were gone, we cleaned up all the messes left behind.

After we were finished, we walked up the stairs and looked for Milroy. We walked together through the halls, and when any patient saw Ben, they ran away from their doors. Ben smirked, claiming he loved tormenting everyone here. He asked how I felt about it. I told him I just like helping people. Ben laughed at me, and then we entered Milroy's office.

Milroy was on the phone when we entered. He glanced at us and held out a figure. We stood there listening to him talk on the phone about some family wanting to send their daughter for being mentally ill, another classic patient. Milroy told them he would see them soon before he hung up. He turned around and looked at us, "Well, tell me. How did everything go?" Ben cleared his throat and told him they were untreatable; they all died when they went through operations. Milroy went quiet and asked how we would dispose of the bodies. I told him that we threw them all in the furnace. A grin formed on Milroy's face. "Well then, I guess there is nothing to worry about." Milroy claimed he would just say they all committed suicide.

Milroy instructed us to go back to work and to fix any patients we wanted. So we both left his office and went our separate ways. I strolled down the halls and saw other nurses wheeling patients to and from the operating rooms. I didn't feel like "fixing" anyone else today, so I made my way to the nurses' chamber. On the way back, I saw Milroy walking with a rich looking family. When Milroy saw me, he called for me to come meet our newest patient. I walked down the flight of stairs and met the family. Milroy said they were here hoping we could fix their daughter, Zoe. I asked what her issue was, and they claimed she was rebellious, violent, and mentally unstable. I assured them we would fix her. The mother smiled and said she would be right back with her daughter.

Milroy watched as the woman walked through the heavy doors. He waited until the doors closed before he grabbed my collar. He whispered in my ear that this was our wealthiest client yet, and he wanted me to be Zoe's only nurse. He informed me that if I failed, then he would let Ben try. I nodded my head, claiming I understood.

The doors squeaked open, and the mother walked back inside. She stepped aside and told us this was her daughter Zoe. The moment I saw Zoe, my heart pounded, and I began to sweat. She was the most beautiful girl I had ever seen. Milroy introduced me to her and informed Zoe I would be the nurse responsible for her. She looked up at me and smiled, followed by a wink.

I grasped Zoe's hand as I led her down the hallways. I felt her eyes pierce through the side of my head. Finally, we got to her room. I unlocked the door and told her this was where she would be staying. She glanced inside and argued she was not going to stay in such a shitty room. I told her that she didn't have a choice, and I shoved her in, locking the door behind her. She swore at me as I walked down the hall back toward the nurses' headquarters.

It was a long night. I had a hard time falling asleep as visions of the foul acts Ben committed played through my brain all night; however, I did eventually fall asleep. I woke up late apparently; all the other nurses were already gone. I quickly sprang out of bed and raced to Zoe's room. When I got there and saw that she was gone, I began to freak out. I started running to other nurses, asking if they'd seen her. No one knew. I began to swear and slammed my hand against the wall.

A patient heard my concerns and informed me they saw Ben take her to an operating room just a few minutes before. I thanked the patient and told their nurse to go easy on them today. I ran like a bat out of hell, barged through the doors of the operating room, and there they were. Ben had just finished retraining Zoe. He looked at me and told me to leave since he was about to perform a lobotomy. I told him no, that Milroy put me in charge of her, and that I would treat her with what I thought was necessary.

Ben told me that wasn't going to happen and reached for an ice pick. I saw tears stream down Zoe's face as he shoved a sock in her mouth so she couldn't scream. Just as Ben grabbed the ice pick, I jumped on his back, attempting to choke him. He ripped me off his back and slammed me on the ground. He stabbed my knee with the ice pick and stepped on it. It tore through my leg. I screamed while he turned back toward Zoe. He swore at me that now he would have to go get another tool kit. He kicked me in the face on his way out.

I waited until the doors closed before I used all my energy to push myself off the ground. I grabbed the side of the chair to pull myself up. I held up a finger to Zoe's lips, telling her I would get her out of here. I looked at the tool kit and grabbed a saw. The doors flung open behind me, and Ben put his hands around my neck. He began choking me, but I managed to smack him in the head with the saw.

He released me and grabbed his ear as it was bleeding. I ripped the ice pick from my knee and hobbled towards Ben. I shoved it through his eye, and he began to scream. He yanked the ice pick from his face, ripping his eye out with it, but he wasn't finished yet. He stumbled towards me, so I turned back to the cart of tools and threw it at his legs. He collapsed on the ground, but with all the tools underneath him, I had nothing to use. Zoe started frantically kicking, so I moved toward her and removed the cloth from her mouth. She told me that in the bottom of her shoe there was a switchblade; she begged me to use it.

Just as I turned back to Ben, he was standing up and had the whip in his hands; he struck me across my face several times, and I began to lose my vision. One of the times he whipped me, Zoe was able to grasp the whip. She tangled it in her restraints, so when Ben yanked on it, it snapped off her wrist restraint. She quickly reached for her shoe, drew her switchblade out, and threw it directly at Ben's face, hitting him in his other eye. I quickly removed the rest of Zoe's restraints, but she didn't want to leave. She told me to grab one of Ben's shoulders and place him in the chair.

I put the restraints on Ben while he squirmed in the chair. Zoe then grabbed the saw off the ground, and began sawing his neck. It was at that moment I realized she really was insane. As she went crazy, severing Ben's head from his body, I wrapped layers of gauze around my leg and found a clean shirt. While I was changing, I heard a sickening thud. I turned around, and lying there in all of that blood was Ben's head. Zoe looked at me and frantically began to panic; she claimed Ben tried raping her, but when she put up too much of a fight, he dragged her into this room. I told her everything was going to be ok. I helped her freshen up before I brought her back to her room. Once she was safe in her room, I hit the panic button on the side of the wall. The lights flickered and a siren began screaming. Half a dozen nurses approached me, and I pointed to the operating room.

Milroy called me in his office and asked me what happened. I told him some of the truth but left out a few things. I told him how I went to Zoe's room and she was missing. I found her in the operating room with Ben trying to perform a lobotomy. I told him to stop because she was my responsibility. I told him how Ben demanded I leave, but when I didn't, he attacked me. I told him it was all in self defense and my inner demons took over. He asked me about the severed head. I told him that Zoe managed to get free from her restraints, grabbed a saw, and cut at his neck.

Milroy sat back in his chair. I could tell he was thinking. He told me he was relieved that I stopped Ben, but he wasn't so happy that Ben was dead. However, Milroy understood Ben's tendencies, so he didn't punish me. He just reminded me to do whatever it took to protect Zoe.

2004

Ryan -

The ward towered over us and made me feel like it would consume us, but I decided we would enter anyway. The main entrance was boarded up, so I kicked the boards until they cracked. Eventually, they broke, and I was able to yank the boards from their posts.

I held Fiona's hand as we entered the asylum. It was awfully hot inside, but I wasn't going to complain; we would rather be warm than cold anyway. We looked around and saw walls fallen over, stairwells dismantled, and ceilings collapsed. Fiona asked me if I was sure we wouldn't get killed going in. I told her not to worry, and I pulled her along, managing to climb up what was left of the stairs to the second floor. The first door we came to had the name Milroy on it. I tried to push it open, but it wouldn't budge, so I slammed my body into it, but it still wouldn't budge. Fiona suggested we just keep moving, but I told her no. As I ran into the door with all my strength, the door fell off its hinges.

Fiona -

The deeper we got into this place the more I felt that we weren't alone. It didn't help that Ryan was making so much damn noise trying to get into a room. I asked if we could just keep going, but he told me no and ran full speed into the door, causing it to fall off its hinges. I rushed inside to make sure he was ok. As I was checking on him, I felt a stinging breeze brush against my back. I turned, and out of the corner of my eye, I swear I saw a face. I screamed and climbed over Ryan.

Ryan groaned and picked himself up off the ground. He asked me why I screamed. I told him I saw something and that we should leave. He reassured me that it was just my mind playing tricks on me. While he was making me feel crazy, a phone rang. It came from behind Ryan. It was an ancient looking landline with its wires cut from the outlet. Ryan had no explanation.

He went to pick it up, but I told him not to. He looked at me and asked, "What's the worst that could happen?" He picked up the phone, but when no one was there, he put it back down. I looked toward the door and saw a figure standing there in scrubs. I screamed bloody murder. Ryan looked at the door and swore. He couldn't believe his eyes. Ryan told the psycho to back off, and just like that, the figure turned around and walked into the hallway.

Ryan looked at me, wide eyed. I told him we were leaving, and he agreed, but once we got out of the room and moved back towards the stairs, there was a large man in scrubs; he was holding a whip and handcuffs. We screamed and ran down the narrow halls, hearing footsteps only a few feet behind us.

1904

Zach -

The year 1904 is when my feelings for Zoe really grew. After Ben's death, the patients seemed to improve better than before. I was now the head nurse. I did my best to make sure patients were getting better; of course, we still used our previous methods, and there still was abuse, but I turned a blind eye to it. I only cared about Zoe.

I started to bond with Zoe. I learned more about her. I did see why she was sent here because there were a lot of things wrong with her; however, underneath all those issues, I saw a beautiful soul. I was determined to help her. I had to.

She told me about her life and the things she did. When she was seven, she had smashed a rock over a sea gull's head because it was stealing her crackers at the beach. When she was eleven, she stabbed her father in the ribs. When she was sixteen, she killed a boy who tried to rape her. Then when she was nineteen, she started hanging out with bad people and got into bad things. She told me how she stole from her parents and would break things if she didn't get her way.

I asked her why she did all these things, but she claimed she didn't know. Eventually, she got sick of me just talking to her. She looked at me and said, "You're supposed to punish me right? Well, why don't you grab the whip right there and whip me?" I told her that was unnecessary, but she begged me, so I complied. I whipped her and she began to moan.

2004

Ryan -

I wished I would've just listened to Fiona because now there was some psycho chasing us. We had no idea where we were going. There were dozens of rooms on either side of us. We ran so fast that Fiona didn't see the leg of a wheelchair, which caused her to trip and fall. Fiona cried that she couldn't feel her leg. I told her that she needed to forget about her damn leg. We were being chased by a psychopath! I helped her to her feet and helped her walk. I glanced behind me but didn't see anything. However, once I looked back in front of me, I saw what looked like a dead person being pushed in a wheelchair by another person in scrubs. I yelled and decided I was going to just carry Fiona; we needed to get out of here.

Fiona moaned that her leg was hurting, so I picked her up and looked around, but all I saw were hallways. Fiona pointed out to me what looked like an exit. It said basement. I didn't care. I ran towards the door and carried Fiona down the stairs. There were several rooms that looked like jail cells. I noticed a bed, so I carried her over and set her down on it.

Just as I placed her on the bed, the door shut behind me. I snapped my neck around and saw the lights were flickering, and I saw the man who was chasing us dragging people by their collars into a room that said operation on it. Moments after he dragged patients in there, there were blood curdling screams, the sounds of bones breaking, and what sounded like the crack of a whip.

1905

Zach -

1905 was one of the worst years at the Milroy asylum. Patients just flooded our system, and we had no room for all of them. I was instructed by Milroy to have the nurses execute patients who had no hope, but even then we still struggled to keep up.

1905 was also the year Zoe got deathly sick. I was very worried about her, but for the sake of the entire ward, I had to isolate her. I snuck her snacks and warm soups when I could, hoping to bring down her fever. I was there for her whenever she needed me.

1906

Zach -

In 1906, Zoe recovered from whatever illness she contracted, and our relationship grew. I will admit we did certain treatments for pleasure, but I really did love her for who she was. Every time her family came to visit, they were impressed by how much Zoe was improving.

However, with Milroy exceeding the asylum's maximum capacity, it forced me to spend less time with Zoe and more time with other patients. I tried to have other nurses take my spot, but Milroy wouldn't allow this.

I tried my best to continue seeing Zoe, and I did, but no matter how hard I tried, I just had less and less time with her.

1907

Zach -

The overwhelming number of patients consumed my time. Zoe started to get worse again, and when her family came to visit, they were often disappointed; however, they kept paying because they had seen the change in Zoe earlier, and they hoped to see that change again.

Every time I was able to get to see Zoe, she seemed more and more depressed. I swear she was no longer even happy to see me. When I confronted her, she just said, "Why bother getting excited? You only spend a few minutes with me a week." She accused me of losing feelings for her. I told her that the opposite was true, but she yelled at me, saying if I really loved her, I would see her more often. I tried to explain everything to her, but Milroy appeared down the hall, so I told Zoe I loved her and that I would make more time for her.

2004

Ryan -

I wasn't sure which was worse, being trapped in the basement with a killer or the sounds I heard coming from the operating room. I first focused on helping Fiona with her leg since there was no way I could kick down these rusty metal bars.

All of a sudden everything went quiet, and the man exited the operating room. He made his way to our cell and opened the door. He grabbed me by the throat, and I saw his name tag; it said Ben. I squirmed because I couldn't breathe. Before I passed out, I heard a crunch. The man dropped me and held his bladder. Fiona said she kicked him in the balls. While he lay there, we ran back up the stairs and out of the basement.

1908

Zach -

I made more time for Zoe; however, I'm not proud of how I did this. I started using the most painless methods of executions on treatable patients so I would have more time to talk with Zoe.

Once again, Zoe began benefiting from our improved relationship, and her parents definitely saw it at their last visit. I was tempted to tell them what was really going on here. I would have loved nothing more than to sign her release papers and get her out of here. I really did love her more than anything. Of course she was crazy, but there was something about her condition that made me attracted to her.

However, since Zoe was so crazy, it made it really hard for me to keep her out of trouble. Whenever she got the chance, she would start brawling with other patients or nurses. She spent a lot of time in the box, the room we send the misbehaving patients to who are too valuable to operate on. One day, Zoe pushed her luck and attacked Dr. Milroy. It was a day that I was supposed to look after her, but I just couldn't get away from my other duties.

According to Milroy, he unlocked her door, and she was rocking on the floor. Since she was such a valuable patient due to her family's wealth, Milroy made sure she had time out of her room. He claimed he was going to bring her to the arts and crafts room when she dug her nails into his eyes. Milroy shoved Zoe to the ground, and stomped on her face; however, he remembered he couldn't kill her, so he called some nurses to bring her to the box.

I made sure to visit her that night, and I got her side of the story. According to Zoe, Milroy took her to an operating room and performed electrical stimulation. I was furious at this, but it got worse. Zoe told me she remembered feeling Milroy touching her after the therapy, and she couldn't move. I grabbed Zoe's hand and kissed it. I promised I would get her out of here.

2004

Ryan -

Once we were out of the basement, I looked around and used anything I could to barricade the door. After I was confident that we had escaped, I turned around to Fiona to check on her, but Fiona was frozen in place, staring at a girl with long ginger hair, wearing a gown and white socks. She had blood stains all over her body. I didn't know whether to feel scared or not as she just stood there, but she answered my question real quick as her jaw dropped open and she screamed, charging at us with a screwdriver.

Fiona -

While Ryan was barricading the basement door, I noticed a thin figure covered in blood stains holding a screwdriver. I stared at her, too afraid to speak. The next thing I knew, she charged at us while screaming.

The bitch tackled me and tried stabbing me in the face with the screwdriver, but I dodged it. Ryan kicked her off me, and she went flying but quickly got back to her feet. She grabbed a pair of scissors off the ground and charged at us again. Ryan stepped in front of me, preventing her from reaching me, but she managed to stab him in the chest. Blood danced down Ryan's shirt, and then my fight or flight kicked in. I yelled and charged at the psychopath.

While we were wrestling, I saw the screwdriver that she dropped when Ryan kicked her. I grabbed it and jammed it into her neck. She shrieked, so I kicked her in the face. I quickly turned my attention back to Ryan, and I helped him regain his balance as we walked up the stairs. I struggled to carry Ryan's weight, so we took a short break. While I was catching my breath, I saw a room that said nurses only on it.

Fearful that the crazy lady would come back, I put Ryan's arm over my shoulder, and we shuffled into the room.

1909

Zach -

Getting Zoe out of Milroy was going to be a challenge, so it took me months to come up with a plan. Yet I finally did. The plan was simple, but it was crucial that it was executed to perfection. The next time Zoe's family came to visit, I slid them a folded up note with the details of what really went on in the Milroy asylum. In the note, I begged them to alert the authorities. I also wrote, "DO NOT TELL DR. MILROY ABOUT THIS!"

The next step was to sign Zoe's release papers and get her out of here. So I strolled into Milroy's office, asking for the key to the drawer of patient release forms. He stared at me, asking whom I planned to release. I told him it was a patient we just got, someone by the name of Bella. He looked at me for a few more seconds and then gave me the key.

I took the papers back to my "office" and filled them out. While I was filling them out, I was startled by the fire alarm going off. Thinking it was real, I left the papers and ran to Zoe's room. Once I got there, I realized there was no fire. I informed Zoe that I almost had her out of here. She smiled, kissed me, and asked how I was going to get out. I told her I'd quit after her release, and we could start a new life together.

Just as quickly as the happiness consumed me, it was replaced with fear. I heard Milroy's voice behind me. He held the release form papers in his hands and confronted me. I didn't know what to say. Milroy shook his head; he claimed this wasn't happening. I cleared my throat and told him that I was going to sign Zoe's release papers, and I would quit afterwards. I told him how I already alerted the authorities. Milroy's facial expression completely changed. He frowned and said that was a mistake.

Zoe -

Just as I thought Zach and I were going to get out of here, Milroy showed up. Zach told him everything and said that we were going to be leaving. I watched Milroy's face scrunch up with disappointment; he told Zach that was a big mistake and drew a pistol from his pocket.

My eyes went wide. He pointed the gun at Zach and shot him five times. Tears washed down my face as I held Zach's hand. I looked up at Milroy and told him I was going to kill him. He told me I didn't have to. I screamed at him, asking what the hell he was talking about. I then watched as he lit a cigarette and tossed it in a laundry bin. As the building was engulfed in flames, he told me he would see me in hell.

2004

Fiona -

We made our way into the nurses' headquarters, and I helped Ryan sit down on a rusty bed frame. I frantically searched the room, hoping to find anything to slow down the bleeding, but I couldn't find anything. Something then tapped me on my shoulder, and I turned and saw the bloody woman behind me. This time she was holding a hammer. Before I could react, she bashed it on the side of my skull. I fell to the ground, my vision blurry.

Ryan -

I must have passed out because when I looked around me, I was in some operating room. I tried to move, but I was chained to a table. I turned my neck and I saw an empty chair. I began to cry because I thought Fiona was gone, but then the doors flung open. A male nurse with brown hair and several gunshot wounds had Fiona in his arms. He tossed her in the chair next to me and restrained her. She was out of it; blood saturated her hair, making it look bright red.

The male nurse then stood still, staring at us, and then the doors flung open again. It was the bitch that was attacking us earlier; she was carrying a long sharp knife. She giggled, noticing I was awake. I then watched her walk towards Fiona, and she jammed the blade underneath Fiona's eye. I will never forget Fiona's blood curdling screams. I felt useless because I couldn't move. Tears trickled down my face. The woman then turned towards me; the male nurse behind her handed her a saw. She kissed him and walked towards me with the saw in her hands and screamed, "If we can't be happy, nobody can!"

Stay Out Of The Attic
Story Summary

The world consists of many dangerous things; they can be anywhere or be anyone. Some may be obvious, while others may be hidden. However, you would probably agree that you're safe from those dangers if you're in your own house. Well that's what Brody thought, too.

Brody -

My father died when I was just 9 years old. I had just reached the age where I had started to understand what death really meant.

As a result of my father's death, my mother took the responsibility to try to act as both my mother and father. I would love to give her credit because she did a great job. She always put me first. I was always her top priority.

My mother always preached the importance of safety. Since she was my only parent, during all of her spare time she was working. This left me home alone a lot since she didn't trust babysitters. Every day, my mother practiced with me how to be safe. If I ever heard a knock at the door, I would never answer. If the phone rang, I never answered. I was also told to never look out the window or have the TV on too loud.

Anyway, I followed my mother's rules for several years, but eventually, I became bored from being alone so much. When I turned 17, I got a job at the local grocery store, which helped me get out of the house and see the real world. Although I will admit, my mother was not wrong about the danger outside the house. While working as a cashier, I saw my fair share of creepy and violent customers.

I can recall a time where a little old woman proceeded to check out with one item. She always got one thing, and it was a knife. You may be wondering why I find this weird; well, every time she came in, she had cuts all over her body, which I assumed were from the many knives she had purchased.

Another customer I remember was Big Bill. Big Bill was a jerk. He never felt like waiting in the line, so he would cut anyone and everyone, and if you bothered protesting, you would get knocked out. I can recall at least four times where this man assaulted other customers for objecting. The only reason I know his name is because he always shouted, "Move it! Big Bill coming through."

I've also seen a lot of things on my walks home from work that I would be happy to forget. I saw everything from drug deals to people getting the life beaten out of them.

Nearly every time I made it home, I was alone, and I was responsible to fend for myself.

Power Outage

Brody -

I was just waking up to go to my 4 PM shift when I was startled by a loud thud. Curious what the noise could've been, I roamed around the house calling for my mom, but she never answered. I looked at my phone; it was 3:30 PM, which meant it was time to leave. Right as I was about to leave for work, the lights flickered and the power went out.

Just moments after the power went out, I heard a series of what sounded like footsteps coming from the attic. I began to shake nervously. I was scared, but I also didn't want to leave the mystery for my mother to discover.

I called off "sick" from work, and I went to the kitchen and reached for a steak knife. I used my phone as a flashlight as I roamed around the house. I didn't find anything. Of course, just as I began to relax I heard it again, but this time it sounded like something was running above me.

I stood frozen in place and looked up at the attic. I shouted, "If anyone's up there, reveal yourself now!" There was no answer. I began sweating profusely as I reached for the attic door. I pulled on the string and backed away while the wooden door opened. I shined my flashlight up into the attic and saw nothing, so I grabbed hold of the old wooden ladder and climbed up into the attic.

I stealthily walked around, trying to be as light on my feet as possible so the floorboards wouldn't creak. Still I saw nothing. Just as I let my guard down, a mouse squeaked and ran across the floor and under my legs. I turned and watched the mouse scurry away. After the critter was out of sight, I brought my attention back in front of me. My soul nearly left my body. I was face to face with some skinny pale creature with intimidatingly large teeth. It cocked its head at me, and I watched blood drip from its mouth. I screamed and ran.

As I ran, I heard the creature crawl behind me. I made it to the attic door and began to climb down the ladder. Just before I was halfway down, the creature grasped my arm. It growled and swung its claws at me. I dodged its swipe, quickly raised the knife, and stabbed its hand. The creature squirmed as the knife pierced through its hand into the wooden floor board.

As the creature was struggling, I slammed the attic door shut. It must have hit the thing in the face because blood oozed from the cracks above.

I raced away from the attic door and went to call the authorities, but I realized I didn't have my phone. I cussed as I realized it was lying in the attic.

I tried using the landline phone we have in our kitchen, but the line was dead. I didn't know what to do. I couldn't contact anyone, and I sure wasn't going to let this thing get away. I grabbed a metal bat from under my bed, sat right underneath the attic door, and waited.

I must have fallen asleep because suddenly, I was awoken by my mother. She asked me what the hell I was doing sleeping with a bat in the middle of the hallway. I was confused because everything seemed normal. The power was back on and everything. I scratched my head, then told her everything from when I woke up to when I escaped the attic.

Her face twisted with what looked like consternation, and she asked if I was feeling ok. I began crying because she didn't believe me. She asked if I went to work, and I told her no. She looked at me, calling me by my first name and telling me I can't just not go to work. I yelled that I was just trying to protect her! My mother sighed and ripped the bat from my grasp. She announced she was going to go up there and kick out the "monster." I erupted, telling her not to go up there, but she went anyway.

Just a few moments after she entered, she screamed. I sprung off the ground and hurried up the ladder. "Mom!" I called. I used her phone as a flashlight to look for her. I eventually found her standing in the corner. I noticed her gaze was glued to the floor boards. She yelled that we had mice. I forgot to mention my mother has a phobia of small rodents because she was bitten by one as a child. Her hands shook as she pointed towards the pool of blood the mice lay in. At that moment, I began to question myself. Was I just imagining it all?

I decided to act like the man of the house the way my dad would've. I reached for my mother's arms and helped her down. I brought her to her bedroom and tucked her in. I told her it would be all right while she shook with fear. As I was attempting to calm her down, I heard a thud followed by what sounded like bones popping out of place. I felt my skin go pale. I slowly turned around and looked out her bedroom door. I saw nothing, but I closed my mother's door in an effort to keep her safe. I raised the bat and began to look around.

I first checked on the attic door; it was wide open. I froze, trying to remember if I left it like that. I turned around and saw a shadow of something galloping into my room. Just then my fight or flight kicked in, and I chose to fight. I yelled as I ran towards my room with the bat, but once I got inside there was nothing there. Confused, I turned back around and heard what sounded like a doorknob juggling. I stuck my head in the hall and saw the damn creature. It was standing on its hind legs like a human, attempting to get into my mother's room.

I violently charged the creature and bashed its head in with the bat. The creature collapsed on the ground and stayed completely still. Just as I believed the nightmare was over, I heard another thud followed by the snap of something wooden. I turned behind me and saw another creature! This one was very small, like the size of a medium sized dog. The little creature hissed and charged at me. I swung at it and missed. This smaller one was too fast. It crawled along the ceiling above me. I looked up and watched it release its grip; it began to fall and landed right on my face. The son of a bitch, scratched my eyes repeatedly. I tried to rip it from my face, but it had a firm grasp around my neck.

I used all my might to finally yank the demon off me. Blood ran down my face, and it felt very warm. I began feeling the side of my head, and I couldn't find my ear! Only able to see out of one eye, I looked back at the dead creature, and saw the little one nearby, munching on my ear. I accepted the fact I was going to die because the abnormal amounts of blood I lost caused me to feel dizzy. However, I decided I wasn't going down without a fight, so I stumbled towards the creature, and I swung at it, but I missed again. I regained my balance as the creature began climbing toward my mother's door. I raised the bat high, and as I was swinging, my mother's door opened and the creature pounced on it, leaving my mother defenseless in the doorway.

It all happened so fast, the bat fractured my mother's skull, and she immediately collapsed on the ground, pools of blood forming around her. I was frozen in place as I watched the little creature crawl towards my mother and begin feasting on her body. Rage consumed me, as I watched my mother's face disappear from her skull. Using the last of my energy, I heaved the bat above my head and brought it down on the small creature. I heard several bones crack as the bat made contact. If I had to guess, I must have repeatedly bashed the thing for hours because I didn't stop until the daylight glared through a hallway window.

I stood still and turned my attention towards the sunlight, and when I turned back and saw what was left of them, I dropped the bat and began to sob. I had to face the realization I had no parents. I had to figure out where I would live. Go figure, my mom was not close with the rest of her family members, so that didn't help. Left with no other options, I called the authorities. They must have thought it was all a joke because they mocked me and said my story was probably just a dream. I had to threaten to harm myself to get them to take me seriously and come to my house.

I watched from the window as only two cop cars arrived and only one officer came and knocked on the door. Not even a second after he knocked, I unlocked the door and opened it. The officer looked at me, and before I could say anything, he began telling me how it was illegal to prank call the police station. I shouted that I was not lying, and were it not for the smell of death in my house, I doubt he would have entered. The officer drew his pistol as he walked through the house. I'd say a minute later I heard a scream, and I heard the officer's shaky voice requesting all available units. Immediately, the officers sitting outside sprang out of their vehicles. They brushed past me with their weapons in their hands. Once they were out of sight, I decided to just walk out and get as far away from there as I could.

Five months later

It's been hard living on my own, but I've been able to make ends meet. I got a job at a nearby hardware store, and I make just enough to be able to afford an apartment. The apartment isn't the nicest of places, but I didn't have much of a choice. At least my job isn't too bad. I get more everyday customers than I did at my old job, and hardly any psychopaths. I work around 40 hours a week, so most of the customers know who I am and always leave good reviews.

Today I was working my last shift of the week from 3 PM to 11 PM on a Friday night. It was just me and two other workers. At about 8 PM, the store started to die down. One of the workers suggested that she should leave earlier since there was supposed to be a bad storm within the hour, and she had to go home to make dinner for her kid.

Honestly, I didn't really care. The store was pretty empty, and my other coworker, a total workaholic, would make sure everything was done before we closed.

At around 10 PM, the storm began. The rain bounced off the store windows, the wind was blowing small things around outside, and there was a lot of loud thunder. I wasn't scared, not one bit, but of course, just as I thought that, the power went out. I reached for my radio and contacted Steve, my coworker. Steve told me to lock up while he checked the circuit breaker.

I told him to be careful while I locked up the store. I radioed Steve back after I locked the door, but he didn't answer, so I tried contacting him a few more times. Still I heard nothing, so I began shouting, "Steve!" I walked around the store looking for the flashlight section, grabbed two heavy duty flashlights, and made my way to the back of the store. I called Steve's name again, and I heard footsteps. I followed the sound of the footsteps, which led me to a ladder. The sign next to the ladder indicated the circuit box was up in the attic of the store.

I felt the hair on my arms crawl as I began climbing the ladder. I shouted Steve's name again, but only my voice echoed off the concrete walls. I looked around with the flashlight and saw Steve! He was at the circuit box. I made my way towards him, and scolded him for not answering me, but Steve still didn't respond. That made me angry, so I grabbed Steve's shoulder and turned him towards me, but his face was half ripped off, and a chunk of his neck was missing. I screamed and turned around, attempting to get back to the ladder; however, once I turned around I was face to face with the same creature that killed my mother. I screamed as it swung its claws at me.

Prisoner Story Summary

There are so many prisons that contain a mixture of low level criminals and cold blooded killers. Unfortunately, even the best maximum security prisons sometimes fail to hold all the prisoners within their walls, resulting in the creation of a prison like no other: the Prison of Death. It is believed all the records of individuals sent there disappear, since everyone dies inside.

Trial

Julian -

I sat there as the jury whispered in another room. I won't lie, I was completely unremorseful about my actions. So it made sense that when the jury came back, concluding I was guilty, that I really didn't care. The judge shifted awkwardly in his chair, his voice trembling as he raised the mallet. "Mr. Brecken, you have been found guilty of the murder of fifteen people, and I hereby sentence you to life in prison without the possibility of parole." There was a brief pause before the mallet kissed its coaster.

I can recall my lawyer telling me the fight was over. I looked him straight in the eyes and whispered, "It's not over until I say it's over." Before either of us could speak another word, I was violently grabbed by several officers and escorted out of the room. I cackled on my way out; it brought me pleasure to make people feel uncomfortable. One officer told me to shut up, so I teased him, claiming he was just scared of me. The officer smirked and said he was terrified as he sucker punched me in the face and shoved a cloth in my mouth to keep me quiet.

I was loaded on a bus with bars replacing windows and brought to the "Maximum Security Prison." I decided to make things difficult for the officers, so I refused to move from my seat. They murmured that someone had to move me. Then this big tough-looking guy took his baton and bashed me on the head. I felt very dizzy, but I can remember people carrying me inside.

Unfortunately, since I was in and out of consciousness, I didn't see the layout of the prison, making it harder for me to make a plan to escape. Once I fully recovered, I started causing mayhem right away. I got into countless fights with criminals and guards whenever I got the chance. Eventually, as I expected, they grew sick of me and decided to send me to a different maximum security prison out in the middle of nowhere.

The prison they brought me to looked like it was physically impossible to escape from. They had sniper towers at each corner, so if you did manage to run away, they would shoot you on sight. I was too intrigued to be a pain in the ass, so I willingly let the guards escort me inside. As we walked through the long halls, it looked nearly impossible to even come in contact with any other prisoners. They escorted me down the hall and gave me my own room.

While two guards had a firm grip on me, the third stepped away to unlock the door. I began calculating my chances and decided now would be the best time. While the one officer was unlocking my cell, I kicked him from behind in the family jewels. He fell to the floor and cried like a baby. I quickly snapped my head to my right, and bit a chunk of the one guard's forearm out, and while blood gushed from his arm, I spat the chunk back in his face. With one guard down and the other freaking out, I took my free hand and punched the last guard in the face. I reached for his belt, grabbed a taser, and jammed it into his neck. The officer shook like he was doing the worm and collapsed, hitting his head on the concrete floor.

Without hesitation, I grabbed one officer's pistol and scurried through the halls. Just before I made it out the door, I heard a loud, irritating alarm go off. Officers rushed down the halls, and I opened fire on all of them, dropping them like flies. I noticed the doors were only a few yards away. Running like a bat out of hell while being shot at, I fired at the hard glass doors. They shattered, so I jumped through and made a run for it. Once I was outside, I noticed that guards were running to each of the four towers with sniper rifles slung over their shoulders. They aimed and began to fire, and they all missed, except for one. There was one guard, with one sniper rifle that only used one bullet, and the bullet pierced through my thigh, causing me to trip over my own two feet. I lay there in pain while I watched dozens of guards rush towards me. I tried to crawl away, but one guard smacked the back of my head with the butt of his weapon, causing me to black out.

Prison of Hell

Julian -

When I woke up, it was pitch black. I had no idea where I was. I attempted to stretch but chains yanked on my wrists and ankles, causing them to cut into my skin. As I tried slipping through the chains, I was flung like a ragdoll into the air. My body slammed against a shallow ceiling, and I landed face first back on the ground. I felt frantic because I had no idea where the hell I was, and I couldn't see anything, so I had to rely on my hearing to figure things out. While I was listening, I heard what sounded like a motor rumbling, and then suddenly, whatever I was in stopped, and my body bashed against a wall. A feeling of malaise settled over me. My back ached, my wrists were bleeding, and my head felt like it was spinning. Finally, I heard the sound of footsteps approaching. Doors swung open, and there stood only one single man.

I wanted to laugh, but I was in too much pain. The man climbed in the van and freed me from my chains. I looked at him, disconcerted. The guy was huge. He looked me dead in the eyes and told me

"Welcome to hell." I couldn't help but laugh. He grabbed me by the throat and asked me what was so funny. My smirk faded as he tossed me on the ground. I looked up and saw nothing but a small dirt hill. I was coughing up blood when the man grabbed me by my hair and dragged me towards it. He stopped at the mound and banged on it. I heard a series of locks click, followed by the door slowly opening. Wherever this door led, it was pitch back. I couldn't see anything.

I attempted to kick the guard's muscular leg, but it did nothing but piss him off. He just grunted and spit on my face. I heard metal clanking, looked back towards the door, and out came two men; they were heavily armed and very tall. The man who brought me here hoisted me up, and each guard grasped one of my shoulders. The two men began cracking my shoulders while the other man stepped in front of me. He stared at me and spoke: "Here is where you spend the rest of your life. You will be restrained at all times, and any attempts to escape will result in a painful death."

The big guy nodded at each guard, and they dragged me into the darkness. The first thing I heard were the screams. I felt my feet clank down what felt like stairs, each step stubbing my toes. Finally, after what felt like hundreds of steps, we reached what I hoped was the floor. I strained my neck and eyes while attempting to make out anything in front of me. I couldn't see shit, and the dim, flickering light didn't help. The guards continued dragging me down the disgusting halls, and any time I tried resisting, it resulted in agonizing pain.

At the end of one of the filth-covered halls was a rusty door. One of the guards released me while the other struggled to open the ancient door. Finally, the door gave way, making a weird squeaking sound. The one guard turned on his flashlight and took a quick glimpse inside. I waited for one of them to say something, but all I got was a head nod from the guard inside, and then I was thrown inside. I looked behind me, but the light quickly vanished, and I sat there alone in the freezing cold room. There were no lights, no beds, and no toilets in here. This place was inhuman, even for a person like me.

In an effort to keep my sanity, I began counting the seconds passing by to give myself an estimation of what time it was. I figured the sensory deprivation was meant to break us down, and the screams I kept hearing seemed to confirm my suspicion By dehumanizing us, one of us was bound to lose their mind, but not me. I changed my mindset and told myself this place was no different from any other prison; it was just designed by a slightly smarter man with a lack of proper hygiene. I remembered that I had gotten out of every prison I was sent to, so this place would be no different.

Julian -

I felt the sandman begin to work his magic, and I became increasingly tired. I decided that, in order to escape, I should attempt to be well rested, so I carefully felt around in the dark making sure there were no sharp objects present. After concluding my search, I yawned and lay on the cold concrete floor. I convinced myself it was just a cold winter night, and I shut my eyes.

I was surprised when no one woke me. There was no alarm, no guard – I awoke on my own. I thought this was strange. I had never heard or experienced anything like this. It started to make me question myself; however, I convinced myself this was just all part of the plot to get me to lose my mind. I yawned and rose from the cold cement floor. I looked around, but everything was still black.

I shuffled my way to a wall and guided my hands along it, hoping to feel a door. Finally, my finger nail sunk into a divot. I began knocking and I heard a hollow sound. I smirked and began pounding on that door like a madman. Eventually the door opened, and there stood the large guard. He asked why I was smirking. I chuckled, "Because I'm gonna get my way out of this place, and I'm going to kill you!" The guard just stood there staring at me. He grasped his pistol from its holder and shot me in the leg. Blood began gushing from my thigh, and I groaned in pain. I began cursing at him, but he just returned my smirk and closed the door, leaving me in the darkness.

While I felt my blood soak into my uniform, I gathered all my strength and began banging my head on the door while screaming. Just before I lost my voice, the door opened, and the large guard, accompanied by two other guards, stood over me. I managed to give them the middle finger, and I spit in their faces. The big guy nodded his head at each guard, and they both reached for what looked like a taser. While one held me, the other jammed the device into my neck. The electricity poured into my body, causing me to shake like a rag doll.

Right as I was about to lose consciousness, the guard let go of me, and my head banged on the floor. I struggled to move; I was in agonizing pain. I reached my hand to the back of my head and felt a warm sticky substance. It was blood. As I lay on the floor, I figured the guards would just leave me there and close the door, but they didn't. The big man gingerly walked towards me. He squatted down next to me and told me again that I wasn't ever getting out of this place, at least not alive. I craned my neck to face him, and, breathing heavily, I gasped the words fuck you. The guard smirked, spat in my face, and kicked me as hard as he could in the ribs. While I lay there coughing up blood, I watched the door close and the light vanish.

I rolled over on my stomach and pushed myself off the ground. With the little energy I had left, I charged at the door, putting my shoulder into it. I heard a pop, and pain shot through my body. I figured I dislocated my shoulder; however, I gathered all my pain, turned it into rage. and began kicking the door repeatedly. Eventually, to my surprise, I heard a snap, and the door swung open. I looked around, making sure the coast was clear, and hobbled down the poorly lit halls.

The lights flickered, just like my vision. I struggled to see what was in front of me. I wandered all around this damn place, but I couldn't find an exit. Right before I lost hope, I saw a door. I had to squint to make out the words written on it. It said inmates' records. I limped vigorously towards the door and pushed it open. I looked around at what had to be several dozen papers stacked neatly on top of one another. Out of curiosity, I picked up one of the papers and read my name! I scanned the paper for any information, and next to the word status, it said I was dead. I cussed and continued reading; it said my cause of death was suicide.

In a moment of rage, I tore the paper until tiny pieces piled like snow on the ground. I attempted to calm myself and began looking for a phone. I threw papers left and right looking for a phone, but I didn't find one. I cussed and turned towards the door, but I froze in my tracks. I was face to face with the big man and two soldiers. The big guy thanked me for getting rid of my own file for him, but he informed me that, considering the damage I'd done, I should've wished I committed suicide. I looked him dead in the eyes and frowned. I pounced on his chest and dug my nails into his eye sockets. While he screamed, the other guards managed to get a hold of me. However, I bit one's wrist, and I reached for the taser in his belt. While the other guard wrestled me to the ground, I managed to press the taser into his stomach. Electricity shot through his body, making him shake like jingle bells.

While all three of them were down, I stepped on the big guy's chest and grasped his pistol. I shot him right in between the eyes. Blood splattered everywhere, some even got on my face, but I simply licked it off. I turned to the other two guards and fired, relieving them of their duties. I crawled on top of one of the skinniest guards, stripped him of his uniform, and swapped it out for mine. I grasped a knife from my belt, and I gently sliced the guard's skin, and began removing it from his face so no one would be able to tell who it was. Just before I left the room, I heard the static sound of a radio. I picked it up and informed the individual that someone had escaped.

Right as the words escaped my mouth, a blaring alarm screamed through the halls. I told the guard on the radio to station all available guards near the entrance to prevent his escape. I stepped over the deceased, pushed the door open, and stepped into the hall. I had to bite my tongue, so I could walk somewhat normally without moaning. I wandered around the halls, now lit with warning lights, until I found a pair of guards standing next to a heavy door. I approached them and told them they were needed down in the inmate records room. They looked at one another and jogged the hall. I waited until they turned a corner before I made my escape.

I pushed the door ajar, and I couldn't believe my eyes. I saw stairs leading to the outside. Dopamine rushed through my brain, and I hobbled up the steps, making my way to the exit. I pushed the door open and peered outside, feeling the cool fresh air on my skin. I took a step forward, but before my foot hit the ground, I felt something sharp pierce into my lower back. Immediately, I lost the ability to stand, and I collapsed. I wasn't able to move anything but my eyes. I heard a raspy voice, telling me that they weren't done with me as they dragged me away from the door.

Rot In Hell

Julian -

I can't remember much besides being dragged away and watching the light vanish. I figured that my head collided with each step, knocking me unconscious. When I woke up, I was in a room that was lit poorly with the same dim yellow lights. I attempted to move, but my body didn't budge. I looked down and saw I was restrained against a chair. I desperately tried moving my hands, but they just lay there like stone. The only thing I could move was my neck, and then I remembered the knife that had impaired into my lower back. I realized I was paralyzed.

Unsure of where I was, I began to scream, hoping someone could help me. While I screamed, I heard what sounded like someone whistling. Then I heard a door open, and in the corner of my eye, I saw a man in scrubs. I looked at him, my eyes drooping, and he just stared at me and waved his hand. He pulled up a chair and told me he would be right back. When he returned, he was pushing a large table; on it were the three bodies of the guards I had killed. The doctor sat down in his chair, looked at me, and claimed what I did wasn't very nice. Without hesitation, he explained that he believed in fairness and justice.

Therefore, he told me, my death had to be the most excruciating and painful death imaginable. He looked at the guard whose face I had peeled off, then looked back at me. He spoke: "An eye for an eye? A face for a face." I watched as he picked up a scalpel, and rolled over in his chair to me. He told me he was curious to see how long I would live while having my face peeled off. I began spitting and screaming at him, desperately trying to defend myself, but he was unfazed. The man grabbed my face and held it still as he began to slice my skin.

Prison of Death Doctor -

I have no problem admitting I enjoyed every second of this. Julian screamed bloody murder as I sliced his skin open and began peeling his face off. I was disappointed to learn he would only live 30 seconds after his face was removed. I left his lifeless body on the table and went to my computer to fill out his form. Cause of death: suicide. Time of death: 8:56 PM. I printed his file and returned it to the inmate's record room.

When I returned, I noticed Julian was missing from the chair. In a moment of confusion, I reached for my radio; however, before I could grasp it, I felt teeth tear into the back of my neck. I collapsed to the floor and rolled onto my back. There he stood, blood dripping from his mouth. I watched as he mumbled that everyone dies inside. He reached for my scalpel and jammed it in my neck. Before my vision darkened, I saw Julian sprint out of the room, shouting "Everyone dies inside!" I was more concerned with how Julian was able to move than the fact that I was dying. When I lodged the knife into his spine, he collapsed and became paralyzed, so how was he walking, and more importantly, how was he alive?

Thee Embedded

Thee Embedded Story Summary

Everyone has their own hobbies, and some can be more dangerous than others. For Melvin, his hobby is hunting; he's been going with his father ever since he was eight years old. It's not until Melvin moves out and meets the girl of his dreams that he unfortunately finds out just how dangerous his hobby can be.

A New Beginning

Melvin -

I remember it like it was yesterday. I watched from a distance as my father slowly lurked through the shrubs, stalking the lone elk with his rifle angled. His finger hugged the trigger, and he squeezed. The rifle fired, but the bullet just grazed the elk's head. I froze as I saw the elk snap its neck towards my father. It shook its head back and forth and galloped right towards him. As the elk swung its antlers, I watched my father's arms being ripped open. While he was trying to defend himself, he bellowed for me to run! But I just stood still and watched my father struggle.

It wasn't until my father was knocked unconscious that I gathered the courage to act. I quickly reached in my pocket and retrieved a small pistol my father got me for my last birthday. I cocked the gun and aimed at the elk's head. I squeezed the trigger, and the bullet bolted from the barrel into the elk's skull. I sprinted to my dad's side while the elk swayed and collapsed. I smacked my father's face repeatedly and shouted his name. Fortunately, after a few minutes, he began to respond. I crouched down and put his arm on my shoulder and helped walk him home.

The memories continued to flood my brain as I packed my things. My father hobbled into my room and told me to not forget my "lucky gun." He joked, "That gun had an aim of its own, you know." I looked at him and smiled, "Well, maybe I just have better aim than you." My father frowned and reminded me of all the animals' heads and kills he had. I laughed, "Well, I must be a better hunter since I didn't miss my shot on the elk." My father conceded and hobbled towards me; he gave me his great "bear" hug, and he said his farewells, telling me how he would miss me.

He held the old screen doors open for me as I loaded my things into my truck. I slammed the truck shut and gave my dad one last hug. He sniffed and told me that I was all grown up. I patted him on the back and claimed that I would come back to visit. He finally released his grip, and I made my way to my truck. I jumped in the driver's seat and jammed the keys into the ignition. The old thing sputtered as it came to life. I readjusted my mirrors and waved at my father as I drove down the dirt driveway onto the county road.

I took the old dirt country road 85 miles to the nearest highway, where I traveled another 210 miles to Cincinnati to start my own life. The trip had taken around four hours so far. I stopped a few times to eat, use the restroom, and get gas. There was definitely a vast change in scenery. I grew up in the countryside, so seeing all these buildings and people was a little overwhelming. Luckily, I wasn't moving into the city, just using its infested roads to get to my destination. Slowly but surely, the vast numbers of people and businesses eventually vanished. According to my map, I was only about 20 miles away from my new home. The closer I got, the more vegetation and wildlife became present, and it started to really feel like home.

A few minutes later, I finally came to a split in the road, the one on the left looked more like a driveway compared to the one that kept going straight. I eased my foot off the gas and turned left onto the long dirt road. The driveway was a little bumpy, but that really didn't bother me too much. The trees began to subside, revealing a large beautiful log cabin. To my surprise when I pulled in, I noticed a red mini car parked on the side of the cabin. I was confused, so I grabbed my pistol and put it behind my belt while I searched my glove box for the keys. The search quickly became frenetic since my keys decided it would be funny to hide from me. Finally, after nearly tearing apart my car, I found my keys; they were under my seat. I snatched the key, attached it to my key ring, closed the door, and locked it twice.

As I faced the cabin, I took a moment to just listen to the birds' dulcet voices. I took a deep breath and made my way towards the door. I inserted the key, twisted the handle, and pushed the door open. I stepped inside, closed the door behind me, and began to take off my shoes. When I turned around, I was startled to see a beautiful young woman wearing a tight red suit, sitting at my kitchen table and filling out what looked like paperwork. She must've heard me because she immediately got up and pushed her silky black hair aside. She introduced herself as Maggie, and she claimed to be the realtor for the cabin. Maggie said she was just getting all the paperwork ready so I could sign it, and she would be out of my way.

She invited me to sit at the wooden kitchen table and attempted to hand me a pen, but she dropped it, and it fell to the floor. I began to get out of my chair to reach it, but she insisted that she could get it. I couldn't help but watch her as she bent over directly in front of me. She stayed in that position for a few seconds before she retrieved the pen, placed it on the table, apologized, and told me where to sign. While I signed each paper, she reached for my hand and grabbed it, and then began rambling on about the cabin. Once I signed the last paper, I clicked the pen and handed it to her. Maggie then asked me if I was a hunter. I hesitated before admitting I was. She smiled and claimed that this was the perfect place for hunting.

I looked at her and asked why she had asked if I was a hunter, and she just replied, "Because I'm one, too, and the way you presented yourself gave me a gut feeling you were one, as well." I smiled and said, "Well, I'll be damned. I've never met a female hunter!" Maggie giggled and informed me not to be fooled by her professional appearance; she was not afraid to get her hands dirty.

I have to admit I was really enjoying this conversation, so I couldn't help but peek at her ring finger. I noticed it was bare, so I asked her if she was married. Maggie blushed and said she wasn't. She claimed she just hasn't found the right guy yet. Maggie then returned the question, and I told her I'd never even had a girlfriend. The only things I loved were my family and hunting.

Maggie approached me and put her hands on my shoulders; she claimed she was in disbelief that someone as good looking as I was could be single. I assured her that I was indeed single, and I joked around by telling her I was ready to mingle. She batted her eyelashes, and smiled, "Well then, you wouldn't happen to want to go hunting with me some time, would you?" I grinned and told her I'd love to and that I would protect her from any of Mother Nature's pets. Maggie laughed and told me she wasn't the one who needed any protection. Maggie leaned her head forward and lightly put her hand around the back of my head. Our lips collided, and it felt like the Fourth of July. She slowly pulled away from me, grabbed the pen, and wrote down her number. She told me to make sure to text her, and I assured her I would. On her way out the door she glanced back at me; she gave me her congratulations and whispered that she could be more than just a hunter. I watched as she blew me a kiss and shut the door.

I made my way to the door, locked it, and looked out the window as she walked away. I have to admit that she had a very attractive figure. Her hips hypnotized me as she walked to her little red car. I watched to make sure she got in her car safely, and she waved to me as she drove away. Her car was soon swallowed by the nearby trees, and all that was left was some of the dirt her tires kicked up. I continued to stare out the window for a few more minutes before I snapped back to reality. Once the dirt clouds dispersed, I turned back to the kitchen and grabbed the paper with Maggie's number. I shoved the piece of paper in my pocket and went back outside to my truck. As I unloaded my truck, I noticed the sun beginning to set at an abnormal pace, so I hurried to get everything out of my truck. One thing I did not like was being outside at night.

I managed to get all my things into the cabin in one piece. Now before you call me a coward or question how I can be a hunter if I'm afraid of the dark, let me explain. Throughout my years of hunting with my father, we hunted everything from a squirrel to a grizzly. Although my father was a great hunter, he would always explain to me never to hunt at night. He told me some myths and legends, which I never believed, but I interpreted his warning to mean that night was when the hunted became the hunters.

Anyway, that was just my superstition. I resumed unpacking my things and began to make myself at home. When I was all settled, I reached for my phone and entered Maggie's number into it. I had just begun to text her when I heard a clicking sound. I paused, grabbed my pistol, and took a look around. I found nothing out of the ordinary, but I did notice one door that was locked up like Fort Knox. I began to get a weird feeling but convinced myself there was probably a reason behind it. So I went back and finished my text to Maggie. I told her it was a pleasure meeting her and that I found her really attractive. Maggie responded with a winky face emoji and claimed that I was the attractive one, followed by a kissy face emoji.

I can't explain to you the feelings that rushed through my body as we flirted back and forth. I became increasingly infatuated. Just as things seemed to be going in a very positive direction, I mentioned that I saw a door, and I asked why it was so securely locked. Maggie's attitude completely changed; she became incredibly defensive. I apologized for bringing it up, but she didn't respond for the rest of the night. I felt like an asshole, and I convinced myself I had just fucked up.

While I was in the middle of tearing myself apart, I noticed a pair of what looked like glowing eyes peering through my kitchen window. I screamed, raced to my room, and grabbed my pistol; however, when I came back, the eyes were gone.
Sweat droplets slid down my face as I checked every window in the cabin, but I found nothing. That night was perhaps the least amount of sleep I'd ever gotten. I felt paranoid out of my mind.

Shockingly, I did manage to get some sleep as I was awoken by a series of loud knocks at my door. I rolled out of bed, grabbed my pistol, and shuffled to the door. I looked through the window and saw Maggie standing on my porch, so I unlocked the door and pushed it open. Maggie immediately began apologizing for how she acted last night. I told her it was fine, but she insisted it had something to do with some guy stalking her. She was just very on edge.

I accepted her apology and invited her inside. I told her to take a seat, and I asked her if she was ok. She claimed she was fine, but she insisted that she felt really bad about last night and she wanted to make up for it. She smiled and rose from the couch. She then took off her shirt and dropped it on the floor. She asked if I was willing to still make her feel protected. I grinned and said of course. Maggie then turned around and wiggled her hips side to side as she slowly removed her leggings. She stood there completely bare, and she climbed on top of me. It was the best feeling of my life. After that magical day, we began seeing each other more often. We often went on hunting dates and participated in more "adult" activities. Everything was perfect.

Tough Love

For the first few months, Maggie and I went through what people call the "honeymoon phase." We could never get enough of one another, and we couldn't bear being apart. However, I eventually left the honeymoon phase, but Maggie did not. I want to make it clear that I still loved Maggie, but I was just not so childishly obsessed over her. Unfortunately, Maggie began to realize that I was no longer obsessed with her. The first few weeks she tried to seduce me more often, but it didn't work as well as she hoped, and that's when things started to take a disconcerting turn.

Maggie started to become controlling. She began questioning where I was going and demanding to see my phone. Maggie would randomly show up at my work at the dealership and watch me. She would accuse me of talking to other girls and come up with these crazy conspiracies. It wasn't until I found out Maggie had put a camera in my car so she could stalk me that I decided I had finally had enough. I told her one night that she had to pack her things and leave. Our relationship was over.

Maggie didn't take that so well. She became violent, threw things at me, and began breaking my stuff. Concerned for my own safety, I grabbed her and gave her my father's famous bear hug. I attempted to restrain her because I didn't want her to hurt me or herself.

She screamed and stomped on my toe, which allowed her to escape my grasp. She followed up by kicking me in the balls. I collapsed on the floor and moaned in pain. She stepped over me, and I heard her open a drawer. Maggie then climbed on top of me and told me I wasn't going anywhere! I felt something sharp prick my neck, and quickly felt woozy. My vision blurred as I watched Maggie walk away from me. The next thing I knew, everything was black.

The Hunt

I remember waking up and being unable to speak, although my vision quickly became sharp. I could see Maggie talking to a man with long dreads, and part of his face was hidden by a mask. Maggie was just in her underwear and sports bra, flirting with the intimidating man. I watched as they became intimate. I knew at that moment that if I didn't get out of there, I would die. I waited until they were both entangled with each other to make a run for it. I pushed myself off the ground and ran into my room. I caught a glimpse of the scary man as he began to chase me. Thankfully, I was already in my room by the time he caught up. I barricaded the door while I crawled under my bed. Frantically, I rummaged through all the crap under my bed until I finally found what I was looking for, the case that contained my lucky pistol. I grabbed it from its case, loaded it, and put extra bullets in my jeans pocket.

Just as I finished loading it, the man began breaking through the door with an ax. He swung the ax like a psychopath and crawled through the split in the door. He tackled me, knocking the gun from my hands. Then the fucker kicked my pistol underneath the bed and retrieved his ax. He hoisted it high and brought it down toward my neck, but I rolled out of the way. The ax slammed into the floor and got stuck. I used this moment to crawl through the splintered door and make a run for it. Just as I made it out of the bedroom, Maggie was standing there, holding a rifle in her hands. She aimed it at me and pulled the trigger. Fortunately, she missed, and I bolted out the front door.

My fight or flight finally kicked in, and I ran like a bat out of hell into the wilderness. I surrendered my body, allowing the branches to tear into my skin. Eventually my body gave out, and I tripped over a log, falling face first into some shrubs.

As a last resort of defense, my mind enabled my hunter senses. I made sure to lie perfectly still and just listen. I heard branches snap in the distance, followed by the sound of a gun being cocked. I slowly rotated myself so I could see them. I stood no chance if I attempted to run.

I waited until the maniac wasn't looking, and I rushed Maggie from behind. She backed her waist into me and told me she knows I miss her and that I should just surrender. As she tried seducing me, I put her in a headlock and wrestled her to the ground. I managed to rip the rifle from her grasp. I wasted no time as I steadied the focus and aimed right for Maggie's head.

Maggie -

I was breathing heavily as I remembered the pleasure I received from being intimate with Melvin; he was better than all the others. I began to see my life flash before my eyes as Melvin raised the rifle, but as he pulled the trigger, Dakota heaved the ax above his head and brought it crashing down, splitting Melvin's head open. I quickly put my hands over my face while blood spewed everywhere.

Melvin's blood splattered all over us, but I wasn't fazed. I sucked the blood off my hands while my boyfriend, Dakota, helped me off the ground. We were both breathing heavily. I jumped into his arms and we aggressively made out. After several minutes, Dakota let go of me and handed me his ax. He picked up Melvin's body and placed him over his shoulder. Dakota made sure to keep the body in good condition since there were parts of him we could preserve.

Once we made it back to the cabin, I limped towards my room and opened a drawer. I pulled out a series of keys and met Dakota at the locked door. I unlocked every lock and repeatedly yanked on the door. Instantly, we were greeted by the distinct aroma of rotting flesh. I hobbled down the steps, and pulled Dakota's cart of tools next to his butchering area. Dakota tossed Melvin's body on the table and grabbed a butcher knife. I told him to surprise me as he began slicing the flesh from the bones. While Dakota was sculpting my surprise, I grabbed my camera and looked at the picture I snapped of Melvin that one night. It was a shame he was so attractive. Oh well, on to the next guy. I told Dakota not to disappoint me with his craftsmanship. I was going to clean up the mess upstairs and wash my red suit.

I walked up the stairs and smiled. I shut the basement door behind me and put Melvin's picture with the others in the chest Dakota sculpted. I looked around at the mess I'd made, at all the rugs, couches, and curtains made from the previous men's skins. I grinned because this was the house of thee embedded, and none of them could ever leave.

Locked Away

Locked Away
Story Summary

Not everyone is fortunate enough to meet their grandparents before they die. However, if you are lucky enough, you should spend time with them because you never know when they will reach their expiration date. As for John, he is just like all the other teenage boys. He is too caught up in his video games to worry about others. It's not until his father guilts him about not visiting his grandparents that John finally decides to spend some time with them, but once John arrives, he realizes that maybe he should've just kept playing his video games.

Guilt

John -

I was in the middle of playing Madden when my father knocked on my door. I pretended not to hear him because I was too involved in my game. It was tied 27-27 with two minutes left in the fourth quarter. Finally, my dad got sick of knocking and shoved my door open. I could see my father's reflection on my TV; he waved his hands back and forth before he yanked my headset from my head. I screamed at him to go away, but he began talking about how I should visit my grandparents, especially since my grandmother wasn't doing very well.

I mocked him, repeating half of his sentence and filling in the blanks with nonsense. It was at that moment I heard my father take a deep breath. This only meant one thing: I was going to get my ass kicked if I didn't apologize. However, I had one play left in my game, it was fourth and goal from the five yard line, so I didn't respond. I knew I was messing with fire, but I couldn't help it. I really needed to win in my game.

The next thing I knew, right as I snapped the ball, my father firmly grasped my Xbox and ripped it from the wall. My TV connection was broken, and I was accused of quitting so I lost the game. The worst part was I was actually going to win, too. I rose out of my gaming chair and got in my father's face. He smirked and said, "Oh, you're a tough guy, aren't you?" It wasn't his words that directly affected me but his actions. My father backed up, dropped my Xbox on the floor, and began stomping on it repeatedly.

I was livid. With rage flowing through my veins, I shoved my father and yelled at him, calling him every foul name in the dictionary. He frowned and shoved me back, and I fell on the floor. He towered over me and began to sniffle; he told me that my grandmother was really ill and that it would be nice if I visited my grandparents. He told me that they didn't have much time left and that it would be nice if I saw them before they passed away. I replied back with "Well, it would've been nice if you hadn't killed my Xbox"! My father's face contorted with anger as he stared at me down. Then my father sniffled again, giving up his efforts to change my mind. I watched him struggle to look at me. His voice trembled while he said that he was just trying to prevent me from making the same mistake that he had made. There was a long silence. My father just shook his head and disappeared into the hallway.

I sat on my floor, and a wave of guilt washed over me. I looked around my room and saw my Xbox in shambles. Then I repeated my father's words. I argued with myself and decided I would call my grandparents, and I would try to sleep over this weekend. I felt my pockets, looking for my phone, but it wasn't there. I began pacing around my room searching for it, and eventually I found it lying under my bed.

I reached for my phone and looked in my contacts for my grandpa's number. I pressed on his number and called him; the phone rang once before my grandfather picked up. His old raspy voice whispered "Hello"? I hesitated before responding "Hi Grandpa. It's me, John." There was a long pause before my grandpa responded; he asked how I was doing. There was another pause since I am not very good at engaging in conversations. I said I was doing ok and began contemplating whether or not to just hang up.

I glanced back at my shattered Xbox and took a deep breath. I told my grandpa I missed him and grandma, and I told him I was wondering if I would be able to see them this weekend. My grandpa stuttered, saying that they would love to see me. I smiled, and said, "Sounds good. I'll see you tomorrow around lunch time." Grandpa's voice cheered up a little bit as he said, "See you tomorrow, Johnny." Before I could say another word, he hung up. I frowned. I hated being called

Johnny; however, I concluded I could make an exception.

I made sure to inform my father. It didn't take too long for me to find him. He was reclined in his chair in the living room watching hockey. My father glanced at me and paused his TV. Then he muttered,"What, Johnny?" I told him that I called Grandpa and decided to go visit them this weekend. My father smiled and rose out of his chair. He messed with my hair and proclaimed that he was proud of me. He asked me what changed my mind. I told him it was the guilt.

My smile quickly faded as I told him I didn't want to make the same mistake he did. He nodded and patted me on the back, saying, "You're doing the right thing, son." I yawned and announced I was heading to bed, and I planned on leaving around lunch time tomorrow. My father wished me a good night, reclined back in his chair, and unpaused the game. I was walking up the stairs when I heard my father's team score, followed by him shouting "Let's fucking go!" I smiled and made my way to my room. I climbed into my bed, lay flat on my back, and looked directly at the ceiling. The next thing I knew, my vision blurred, my thoughts dispersed, and I fell into a deep sleep.

Long Time No See

John -

I was in the middle of a deep sleep when something abruptly awoke me. I heard my father's voice. He blurted that it was almost noon, and if I wanted to get to my grandparents' at 1 PM, I had better get ready to leave. I groaned and rolled over, muttering that I didn't want to go. My father shook me and told me that I had promised my grandpa I was going to see him, so he suggested I get my ass out of bed and wake up.

I flipped him off, rolled off my bed, and hit my head against the hardwood floor. I rubbed my forehead and felt a bump beginning to form. I muttered to myself, "Great, just what I needed." I stumbled towards my bathroom and went about my morning routine. I even took a cold shower to help wake me up. By the time I was done, it was quarter to one. I swore under my breath, frantically ate breakfast, and ran out the door. I unlocked my jeep and jumped into the driver's seat. I fastened my seatbelt and stepped on the gas. I was racing against time. I really couldn't bear lying to my grandpa. The trees flashed by me as I went over 20 miles over every speed limit. Somehow, I didn't get pulled over.

I looked at my watch; it was five to one. I looked around as I sped through a depressing neighborhood. I glanced at my side mirror and noticed a figure standing in the road staring at me. I thought it was just a drug addict, so I wasn't very frightened. I regained my focus on the road, and suddenly my surroundings became familiar. I saw the old park I used to play at when I was a little kid, but now it was nearly rusted away.

I squinted to make out the street names. I saw a sign that read Trisket Lane with an arrow directed to my right. I smacked my blinker on and made a sharp turn. I glanced back at my watch. It was 12:59 PM. I looked back up and recognized a large old wooden house. It was my grandparents' place. I slammed on the brakes, causing my vehicle to skid. I began pumping my brakes as I rolled up the cracked concrete driveway. Thankfully, my vehicle stopped just inches away from the garage door.

My heart was racing, and I looked down at my watch; it was 1:00 PM. I let out a sigh of relief and turned off my Jeep. As I stepped out, I heard the old plastic door hinges squeak. I quickly glanced at the front door, and I saw my short, sweet grandpa smile at me. His smile was enough to make my day. Using his cane, he hobbled over to me and excitedly yelled out my name. He opened his arms and gave me a big old bear hug. He looked at me and asked how I was doing. I told him, "You know,

I've been working a lot, and I'm going to college, so I'm pretty busy," which was all a lie. There was a short pause before my grandpa insisted I come in. As we walked through the old cracked wooden door frame, my Papa shouted "Susan, guess who's here!" Again, there was a faint silence before there was a response. I then heard my gentle grandmother's voice call out "Johnny?"

I followed my Papa into the living room, and I noticed my grandmother was sitting in a recliner. Her face bloomed with happiness when she saw me. She struggled to get out of the chair, but I told her not to worry, I would come to her. My little old grandmother grabbed my cheeks and told me that I was such an attractive young man. I thanked my grandma, and she asked me the same question grandpa asked me in the driveway. I gave her the same exact answer.

My grandpa hobbled over to the couch and sat directly across from my grandma. They both made very clear how much they missed me. My grandpa started telling me some stories from when I was just a toddler while my grandma found pictures from when I was younger.

I won't lie, it felt very comforting, spending some quality time with them. It pained me to see how wrinkled their skin was. I couldn't help myself as tears started trickling down my face. I gave my grandpa a big hug. Strangely, when I attempted hugging my grandma, my grandpa erupted that I shouldn't hug her as she was not feeling so well. Startled, I stepped back and returned to my seat. There was a short silence. As my grandma craned her neck, my grandpa turned around and looked at the clock. He coughed and asked if anyone was hungry. I replied with a firm yes. He scratched his head and asked if I would like pizza? My eyes lit up with excitement. I love pizza! My grandpa smiled and said good.

I asked him what the name of the pizza place was, and I offered to call them. My grandpa shook his head and said they don't deliver. He announced that he could go get the pizza, but I objected, claiming I could do it so he wouldn't have to drive. My grandpa looked at me and glanced at my grandmother. He insisted I stay here and spend some time with my grandma, especially considering I hadn't seen them in years. I watched my grandfather grab his keys, and he waved as he went out the door.

I heard his engine rumble and watched his headlights shine through the window as he began to pull out of the driveway. I waited until after his vehicle was out of sight before I started a conversation with my grandma. However, when I turned around, she was gone.

Feeling confused, I shouted my grandmother's name. I wandered around the house, but I couldn't find her. I began to wonder whether or not I should call my grandpa. While I was wondering what to do, I heard glass shatter upstairs. I dropped my phone and sprinted upstairs. I heard what sounded like my grandma sobbing in her room. I knocked on the door and attempted to twist the handle before a deep voice called out, "Don't open the door!"

I took a step back, as the voice sounded beyond disturbing. I slowly reached for my phone but then remembered I dropped it downstairs. As I began to make my way down the stairs, my grandmother's door cracked open, and her sweet feminine voice whispered, "I'm sorry, Johnny honey. Can you please go into the guest bedroom and lock the door? I'm not feeling too well." Before I could respond, the door slammed shut. My heart began pounding, and I ran to the guest bedroom. Once I was inside, I locked the door and began barricading it.

I sat on the bed rocking like a child, traumatized by what I had just heard. To my horror, I realized the nightmare had just begun. While I waited for my grandpa to return, I heard a door click, followed by door hinges making an eerie squeak. There was a brief silence before my grandmother's voice echoed, "Johnny, where are you? Can you help me with my medicine, honey?" Each time she repeated herself, her voice deepened to the point where it sounded completely demonic. I saw the shadow of her slippers stop right underneath the door.

I watched as sweat soaked my clothes and the door knob began jiggling. She started banging on the door and screaming, "Let me in!"

Just as I thought I was going to die, I heard the downstairs door open. My grandpa yelled, "I'm back"! Immediately, the banging stopped and turned into gentle tapping. I heard my grandpa call our names, and my grandma responded that we were upstairs. My grandma whispered that it was safe now, and that I should meet them downstairs for dinner. I looked around, grabbed a hanger, and hesitantly unbarricaded the door. I unlocked it and glanced around before letting the door open. When I looked to my right, I saw what looked like a figure's shadow. It slammed my grandparents' door shut. I nearly shit my pants as I ran downstairs into the kitchen.

I was out of breath when I made it downstairs; my grandpa looked at me with great concern and asked if I was ok. I was hyperventilating, and I began spewing out everything that happened when my papa left. There was a long silence. Finally, my grandma spoke, "Oh I'm so sorry, Johnny. I was just looking for my meds, and my voice began to sound raspy." My grandma looked at my grandpa and reminded him that she was out of her meds and needed more. I watched my grandpa's face as it contorted; he looked completely concerned.

My grandpa said, "Well, I guess I'll just have to get you some more tomorrow." He then looked at me and told me to help myself to as much pizza as I wanted because they didn't like having leftovers. Guilt washed over me. I began to believe I had been terribly mistaken about what happened when I was left alone with Grandma. I sat there quietly and munched on my slice of pizza.

My grandma attempted to lighten everyone's mood by suggesting we play a board game or a card game. My grandpa laughed and said that sounded perfect. He got up, left the kitchen table, and went to retrieve a deck of cards. While he was absent from the table, I told my grandma that I was sorry for how I behaved when she was knocking on my door. She smiled and claimed it was perfectly fine. Sometimes it can be weird when you spend some time with your grandparents.

My grandpa quickly returned with a deck, and he dealt everyone their cards. We played for what felt like hours; in total, we played five games. I won once, and both my grandparents won twice. I will admit it was pretty fun. It was almost more fun than my video games. Anyway, once the clock hit 11:00 PM, my grandpa announced it was time to hit the hay. He walked me to my room, which was the room I had been hiding in earlier. He brought me some extra pillows and blankets. He said that if I needed to use the bathroom to just use the one downstairs since the one upstairs was in their room.

Before he closed my door, he informed me that there was supposed to be a storm passing over tonight, so if I heard any loud noises that it was probably just the storm and not to worry. He suggested I also lock my door since my grandmother tends to sleepwalk. Seconds after he closed the door, I made sure to lock the door behind him. I flipped the light switch off, crawled into my bed, got comfy, and fell asleep.

3:00AM

Johnny -

I woke to the sound of the thunderstorm booming. I stretched and yawned and turned towards the clock to see what time it was. The clock read 3:00 AM.

A sudden wave of fear consumed me, and to make matters worse, I heard footsteps in the hallway. I saw the shadows of my grandmother's slippers again as she jiggled the door knob. She began knocking lightly and asked for her medicine. I replied, "Grandma, go to sleep; it's 3:00 in the morning."

I soon realized that was a daunting mistake. As my grandmother began pounding on the door, her voice deepened again. It only lasted a few minutes before I heard my grandpa call her name. Immediately, her voice returned to normal. She claimed she was just getting a drink. I couldn't have been more thankful to hear the sound of their door closing.

I struggled to fall asleep after the incident, so I decided I should go to the bathroom and wash my face. I listened carefully, making sure there was no one in the hallway while I unlocked my door. I took a quick glance around as I made my way down the stairs. Once I was halfway down, I heard my grandparents' squeaky door creak open again, and I heard my grandma's voice. She was calling my name. I was frozen in fear as I watched from the bottom of the stairs. There was a pause, and then out of nowhere, my grandma sprinted down the hallway and into my room.

I began convincing myself I was crazy, so I rushed to the bathroom and dunked my head in the sink, turning on the cold water. Then I slapped myself a few times, telling myself it wasn't real. I took a deep breath and grasped the bathroom door knob. I turned it until it clicked, and then I pushed it open.

The door creaked as it slowly opened. Once I stepped out of the bathroom, my soul nearly left my body as I saw what looked like my grandma at the bottom of the stairwell. Her mouth widened, her voice deepened, and she sprinted at me.

I was able to dodge her initial attack while I made my way to the stairs. I ran up the stairs like there was no tomorrow and raced to my room, but the door wouldn't budge because it was locked from the inside. I began yanking on it, but it still wouldn't budge. As I struggled, I heard the deep demonic voice from behind me. It was laughing and saying, "You're not going anywhere."

I wasted no time. I pivoted to my left and ran into my grandpa's room. I slammed the door shut and turned on the lights. When I turned around, I screamed as I saw my sweet little old grandpa's lifeless body hanging from the ceiling, cords wrapped around his neck.

I began sobbing. I now firmly believed I was going to die. I decided there was nothing I could do but pray. I got down on my knees and began praying to the lord to save me. As I prayed, my grandpa's door began to vibrate; what was once my grandma was pounding on it. Her voice continued to deepen as she demanded I open the door.

I did my best to ignore it as I continued praying. The longer I prayed, the louder the demon got. Eventually, to my surprise, it stopped. The house was still. You could hear a pin drop. I stopped praying and turned around.

Once I turned around, any hope I had flushed away. I saw my grandmother standing over me, smiling with black teeth. Her demonic voice said, "You shouldn't have stopped praying." I was too scared to move as I watched her mouth widen again. She grabbed me, her mouth continued to widen, and she smiled.

Suddenly, my grandmother's normal gentle voice returned. She apologized and told me I should've just stayed home. The next thing I knew, my grandma lifted me off the ground, and she began shoving my legs into her mouth. I tried to squirm away, but she quickly devoured me up to my waist. As her soft gums neared my throat, I looked at my poor grandpa, who was hanging from the ceiling.

Made in the USA
Coppell, TX
30 March 2024

30682880R00152